# THE GHOSTS OF BRISTLEWOOD MANOR

**Also by Percy Popham**

*Providence & Propriety*
*The Officer and the Dandy*

# THE GHOSTS OF BRISTLEWOOD MANOR

A Homoerotic Gothic Horror

*by*

Percy Popham

# AUTHOR'S NOTE

*Dear reader,*

*The following story is very important to me. But as such, it deals heavily with themes of grief and religious trauma.*

*There are also some brief mentions of suicide and domestic violence.*

*Please read with care.*

# CHAPTER ONE

The letter declaring an offer of employment was such a queer, mysterious bit of correspondence that any aspiring tutor in search of a respectable occupation would have immediately passed on to the next.

That, my dear reader, is what you must understand as we begin, and you must bear it in mind throughout the following history. There are times when an uneasy first impression is just that, and the ensuing episodes prove that the initial wariness was unwarranted.

The tale I am about to relate to you was not one of those times. I could never have foreseen the repercussions my answering that missive would produce.

I was inexorably drawn to the letter, even though heretofore I had been one of those aspiring tutors in search of a respectable occupation. However, the strangeness itself was alluring. First and foremost, the nature of the work was extraordinary. And then there was the laconic tone and the childish calligraphy to consider. Finally and outstandingly, the proposed salary of one hundred pounds a year was not something I could regard with anything less than pragmatic avarice. All of those factors induced me to contemplate the offer despite the angst it aroused within me.

For the sake of transparency with my readers, I will replicate here the exact wording of the letter, for I have never let go of it:

*"Dear Sir, I write with respect to your advertisement for the post of tutor. There is no child involved but a man. No further questions will be answered. Pay is one hundred pounds a year plus*

*victuals and board. Please send notice of acceptance to Bristlewood Manor prior to arrival. Signed, Mr. H. Fairfield."*

It was a strange letter, was it not? My mother and father both told me so, and they urged me in no uncertain terms to disregard it immediately. I was, they said, not so desperate that I needed to accept whatever proposition came my way. They would have rather allowed me to live under their roof without any assignment than see me wind up in a substandard situation. As to the salary, they suspected it was a bit of bait to entice some sorry sop into dire straits.

Perhaps they had appraised the situation correctly; I couldn't find any singular flaw in their argument. True, this was the first job offer I had received since advertising my services in the newspaper, and I presumed there would certainly be others of a more reputable character arriving in due time.

And yet, I found myself incapable of tossing it out. For one thing, it was onerous to part with the prospect of one hundred pounds a year – on top of housing and meals – in my first professional opportunity. And for another thing, the fact that there was no child to educate was a winning stroke, if an unusual one; at the time, I served as a teacher at the school I had attended myself once, and that experience revealed to me that I did not much like children, especially the raucous young boys I had the tiresome task of instructing. I needed to escape from the classroom setting, and I'd only decided to advertise as a tutor because, as a third son, I'd liked the thought of joining the church or the military far less. That was much to my parents' chagrin, as my father himself was a vicar, and they both thought a career in His Majesty's service an honorable recourse.

I admit I had never heard of anyone contracting a tutor for a grown man before, and perhaps that should have been some cause for concern. But who was to say there was anything untoward about someone wishing to better himself in adulthood? Self-education was admirable, but it was not necessarily attainable for everyone, even after escaping the ineptitude of childhood.

But there was no denying the line declaring that "No further questions will be answered" and the lack of any petition for references were enough to make me pause, if only for a brief spell. Both parties were within their rights to require more information about the other, and I was never content with unknowing when intelligence was available. I wondered how Mr. H. Fairfield could be complacent enough to content himself without any additional recommendation besides my self-promotion in the newspaper.

Those details, in addition to the slipshod manner in which the note had been scrawled, should have alerted me to the dubiousness of the engagement. And I suppose they did, for I was fully aware of them as I made my decision. After two days of deliberation and against my parents' wishes, I wrote back to Mr. H. Fairfield to announce my assent to his terms and to supply him with my date of arrival. However many misgivings I may have had, there were one hundred convincing arguments per year to countervail them.

Bristlewood Manor, I soon found out, was two miles north of the town of B—, which meant I had to make a half day's journey by stagecoach from my childhood home in L—. I had returned to L— after completing my study at college, and it was there I lived while teaching those odious boys. My mother, in particular, did not understand why I wasn't content to stay at my teaching post, especially when I could sleep in the bed of my youth and surround myself with family.

But, as you already know, I was overwhelmed by my reign over so many children and had been feeling quite squelched while living in my parents' house again. There was a certain thrill in being able to strike out on my own and put some distance between myself and them. I was principally glad to be free of their persistent importuning that I find a wife; I was, by then, quite convinced that I had no want of a woman, and I was tired of feigning an interest in obtaining one.

Fortunately, my parents did not threaten to cut me off or otherwise punish me for accepting the position. They simply made their feelings about the engagement abundantly clear and asked several times if I was certain I wanted to do this. I assured them I was and that if it proved to be a mistake, I would scuttle home immediately and happily confess they had been right all along. That only placated them somewhat, but I was intent on going regardless.

The appointed early summer day then arrived, and I wished them a very fond farewell, kissing my mother's cheek and pressing my father's hand. Then, after promising to write often, I climbed into the stagecoach and decamped from their company.

That was the last time I ever saw my mother alive. She had never, in my recollection, been the hardiest of women, but I had no reason to suspect how rapidly her health would deteriorate after my departure.

The sky was overcast the afternoon I arrived at Bristlewood Manor, casting the worst possible atmospheric backdrop for forming a first impression of the enormous mansion. I had sampled enough horror novels while at college to understand that gloominess was merely a contrived plot device to imbue the reader with a sense of foreboding. In reality, the weather was just the weather; the sun and clouds hovered over beautiful and innocuous residences with as much regularity as they did over the enigmatic and haunted. That thought, while comforting to a point, did not completely divest me of the fretfulness I felt upon beholding the manor. For indeed, the house itself was dingy and austere, and the grounds were not well cared for in the slightest. It was precisely the kind of place in which Mrs. Ann Radcliffe would have set one of her harrowing books.

I tried my best to dismiss those anxious thoughts as utter foolishness, which I was convinced they were anyway. With my trunk of scant belongings in tow, I disembarked from the stagecoach, passed through the courtyard of Bristlewood Manor, and approached the front door. The knock I rapped out seemed to echo ominously. Again, I reminded myself that sounds, in and of themselves, had no moral character and that it was only my mind granting the noise a quality it did not possess in reality.

But there was still a bit of a tremor in my chest, and it had less to do with the anxiety over meeting new people.

After a minute or two, the door opened just far enough for a withered, old hag in a white bonnet, who might have been beautiful once had she not been so hideous, to peer out at me cantankerously.

"Are you Mr. Hayward?" she asked in a voice marked by a high-pitched croak.

"At your service, madam," I replied, offering her an obeisant bow.

The woman did not curtsy in response; she merely gave a quick, backward snap of her head, which was as good as an invitation, and stepped back from the door. I pushed it fully ajar and followed her inside, finding myself in a capacious but dimly lit vestibule. It had been finely ornamented once upon a time; and strictly speaking, it still was, though dust, darkness, and obsolescence had starkly altered its presentation. Had I not known better, I should have believed the tenants had abandoned the place many years ago, leaving it to decay with the passage of time.

"Welcome to Bristlewood Manor," she said with neither warmth nor hospitality, a tone fit for an edifice with an aura such as this.

The lady eyed me as if she was miffed by my presence there, as if I had called unexpectedly — which I had not.

"Thank you," I replied, glancing around at my new lodgings and beseeching the divine to not let this be a grievous misstep. I already felt the urge to sneeze. "I beg your pardon, madam, but I did not catch your name."

"Mrs. Hawthorne," she pronounced matter-of-factly.

"Ah, yes," I replied with a dip of my head. "Well, it is a pleasure to make your acquaintance. Is the master of the house in? I would very much like to meet him straight away."

"Mr. Fairfield is upstairs in his apartment and does not wish to be disturbed until the morrow," explained Mrs. Hawthorne.

Now, that was certainly odd! My response to Mr. Fairfield had precisely stated the day on which I would arrive at Bristlewood Manor, and I knew at least Mrs. Hawthorne had read it or else she would not have known my name when she answered the door. It seemed, at an absolute minimum, rather ungentlemanly of Mr. Fairfield that he did not make time to greet the new tutor.

But I knew I need not have been too shocked. After all, that was by no means the strangest circumstance of this whole affair, and I doubted it would be the last either. Therefore, I told myself, I might as well get used to the eccentricity, and maybe I could even find some delight in it. Besides, I had often felt quite different from my peers throughout my life (for quite consequential reasons that I promise I will elucidate later in this book), and I had adopted something of a contrarian approach to life as a means of self-defense. Perhaps it was that philosophy that had helped guide me to Bristlewood Manor against all better judgment; as someone who appreciated uniqueness, a unique situation (and yes, the money) was too tempting to pass up. As such, I supposed it would not do to despise the bizarre idiosyncrasies of my new associates.

"I quite understand, madam," I told Mrs. Hawthorne, allowing no indication of my disappointment. I was determined to be as ingratiating as possible. "That shall give me an opportunity to get to know the place before I get to know the man, I suppose. And, without a doubt, Mr. Fairfield is a very important man with very important business in need of his very important and undivided attention."

Mrs. Hawthorne made a noise that suggested she found my claim to be only negligibly true. And then she began walking away from me with a hobble, seemingly content to leave me there in the vestibule.

"Uh, pardon me, Mrs. Hawthorne," I called after her. She turned around with an annoyed harrumph. "Is there someone from the service staff who could show me to my room?"

Mrs. Hawthorne laughed mirthlessly. "Service staff? Do you see any other service staff around here? I am the service staff of Bristlewood Manor, Mr. Hayward. And now you are as well, I should say."

I cocked an inquisitive eyebrow at her. "Mr. Fairfield does not employ any others?" I asked, although, based on the derelict state of Bristlewood Manor, I found no great obstacle in believing it. But it was still unprecedented that this large of a dwelling should have only one ancient, surly woman to keep it.

"No," she answered, apparently having determined that any further expounding on the matter would have been superfluous.

I nodded my comprehension of the situation, although I did not comprehend the rationale behind it. "In that case, might I trouble you to show me to my room?"

Judging by Mrs. Hawthorne's outward reaction, you might have surmised I had asked her to carry me up seven flights of stairs on her back. I could sympathize with her to a point; she was elderly and appeared exhausted already, no doubt from the toil of being the lone individual caring for such an extensive mansion – and maintaining that peevish expression. And yet, it could not be helped, unless I was to go poking behind each door in the house and guessing which room I was to take.

She must have come to the same conclusion I had because she said, "I suppose I will if I must. Mr. Fairfield would not want you wandering about the place and snooping around anyhow. And you should know there are only certain places you are allowed to go. You may be anywhere on the ground floor provided that you are not in my way."

The last bit had the ring of a threat.

She moved toward the front staircase, and I pursued her, dragging my trunk along with me. She took each step slowly and with an arduous effort; and so, recognizing this trip up was bound to take a while, I decided to make conversation with my new companion.

"How long have you been employed at Bristlewood Manor, Mrs. Hawthorne?" I asked.

"Since long before you were born," she replied.

I was twenty-three then, and I calculated she must have been nearly three times my age if not more, so that seemed to check out.

"And has Mr. Fairfield owned the home through all that time?" I pressed.

"Not this Mr. Fairfield," she muttered blithely.

"Then, I must assume his father owned it previously?"

Mrs. Hawthorne paused on the steps and fixed me with a stern stare. "I think that is quite enough of your questions for now, Mr. Hayward," she snorted.

I nodded in concession, but my curiosity was far from sated. I had a bad habit of liking to know things, particularly as they concerned my occupational and residential arrangements. This housekeeper seemed to believe there could have been nothing more repugnant than that.

We reached the landing of the second floor. Mrs. Hawthorne stopped there, catching her breath. Then, after a moment, she whispered, "This is where the master's apartment is. He is a very private man. Under no circumstances may you be on this level aside from passing through it to reach the third floor."

"Understood," I said quietly.

With a deep, long inspiration and a look of dread in here eyes, Mrs. Hawthorne gazed up at the next set of stairs. Then, she turned back to me. "The first door on the left is yours," she muttered. "Do not enter any of the other rooms; there is not much to see in them anyway. I do not wish to go up another flight of stairs, so you can show yourself in."

"Thank you, Mrs. Hawthorne. You have been most gracious with your time. " I bowed to her again (she said and did exactly nothing in response), and then I ascended the steps to the uppermost level while she prepared to return to the ground floor.

It was dark up there save for the daylight issuing through the two large windows at either end of the hall. On reaching the door that Mrs. Hawthorne had denoted, I turned the knob and pushed it open. Inside, I found a small room, with a bed placed along the near wall. There was a bedside table beside it with a candle set on its surface. On the far wall, to the left of a modest window, there was a rustic tallboy that had seen better days, though perhaps not much better. A small mirror was affixed to the top of it.

The air was damp and musty, and, as my first home-making task, I crossed the room and threw open the window. That helped with the climate to a degree, although it was evident that Mrs. Hawthorne had not been up here to clean in some time. Dust lingered on everything and cobwebs haunted each corner. Those quarters had the feel of a neglected storage shack more than a bedchamber. But this was my humble abode now, and I briefly felt an impulse to cry at the blessed depth of its humility.

I sneezed, and then I recalled that my salary would be one hundred pounds a year and that already there was a bit of a mystery afoot. In addition, my work in Bristlewood Manor would not require me to teach any pesky, little children or any more than one person at a time. Those remembrances lifted my spirits, and I saw the little room with fresh eyes. Certainly, it would need some touching up here and there and everywhere in between, but that wasn't anything I could not handle on my own, especially with one hundred pounds a year at my disposal.

And there were no parents around to nag me about procuring a wife. And there would never be a wife.

After unpacking my trunk into the tallboy's drawers and setting my Bible on the bedside table, I sat down on the mattress and soon felt the weariness of a half-day's travel come over me. The bed was not as cozy as the one I had slept on in my parents' home, but compared to the veritable pile of bricks on which I had reposed at college, this one may as well have been fit for a king. Still fully dressed and in my shoes, I lay back, set my head on the pillow, and closed my heavy eyelids.

Holding a quick conference with myself, I determined that, if nothing else, this would certainly be a fascinating adventure.

# CHAPTER TWO

When I awoke from my doze, I saw by way of the open window that the evening was already well on its way. That made me wonder what Bristlewood Manor would be like under the shroud of darkness.

Sitting up, I rubbed my still-sleepy eyes. Then I got to my feet with a groan, feeling as if I could have slept for another hour or two. After checking my appearance in the mirror atop the tallboy, I left the room and went to the ground floor to see about supper.

Mrs. Hawthorne had not given me a tour of the main level, and so I had to pass through a few drab, cavernous rooms before finding the kitchen. She was there, standing at a shabby table and arranging a plated meal on a tray.

"I wondered if you would come down to eat," she growled at me, though evidently her wondering was not paired with any concern. "This," she went on, indicating the tray, "is for Mr. Fairfield. I must carry it up to him and leave it outside his door. I would ask you to do it, but Mr. Fairfield would not appreciate that, especially because you are still a stranger to him. You may serve yourself. I have done quite enough by making a sufficient amount for you."

"Very good, Mrs. Hawthorne," I replied. "Thank you."

Saying nothing in response, she removed from the kitchen. I made my plate, scooping up some sort of meat along with hard bread and a mix of vegetables. Sitting down at the table, I took a bite. Well, if that morsel was indicative of Mrs. Hawthorne's cooking in general, then, at the very least, college had granted me plenty of practice at eating flavorless rubbish. And besides, it was not costing me anything, and I was certainly no gourmand. It would do.

By the time Mrs. Hawthorne returned, I had already finished eating. However, I stayed at the table, hoping to talk more with her.

But when she passed through the door, she stopped and glared at me. "That's my seat," she said.

"Oh, I'm so sorry," I said, standing up and moving to the other side of the table.

With a groan, she went to fix her plate and then took up the chair I had vacated, seeming to have decided not to notice my presence in front of her.

I allowed her a few minutes to swallow a bit of her aliments, and then I asked, "Mrs. Hawthorne, might I ask you: what sort of a man is Mr. Fairfield?"

"I thought I told you I'd had enough of your questions," she returned splenetically.

"I do apologize for being a nuisance," I said obsequiously, "but I know so little about the situation I've just stepped into. I feel that in order to do my work to the utmost, it would behoove me to have a little bit more understanding than I do now."

Mrs. Hawthorne glowered at me. Then, she said, "Mr. Fairfield is a very private man, as I told you before, and he keeps few acquaintances because he prefers it that way. He has no patience for a meddler, so it would be best for you to curb your interest before you end up in trouble with him. *That* is the sort of man he is."

"It sounds like he has something to hide," I mused, the sentence slipping out before I had the chance to consider its expedience any further.

"Well, we all have something to hide," she posited.

I did not know if that was a universal verity, but it was true enough in my case. Like Mr. Fairfield, I, too, had a secret, one that befuddled even me. However, I had learned long ago to ignore it outside of my most intimate moments, for it was one of those secrets that would stay dormant so long as I let it sleep.

"And what is it you are hiding, Mrs. Hawthorne?" I ventured to ask, if only to see how she would respond.

"Reveal your mysteries to me first, Mr. Hayward, and then I shall reveal mine to you," she replied.

I smiled at her, a pleasantry she did not condescend to reciprocate. "Then under those circumstances, I suppose it would be best for both of us to keep on our masks," I said.

"For once, I agree with you," she said, though without the cordiality of one who has found common ground with another. "Since you would prefer not to have anyone prying into your business, Mr. Hayward, perhaps you should avoid prying into that of others."

It was a fair exhortation, to be sure, but it did not serve to moderate my inquisitiveness. We may all have something to hide, but there were some people whose secrets were more intriguing than others. Some individuals' mysteries practically begged to be exposed, simply based on how they presented themselves. I did not consider myself of that class, as I was a lowly, young tutor with a congenial enough disposition; who should have cared to know what I kept concealed inside myself? But Mr. Fairfield, on the other hand, was a rich gentleman who lived in a large but tenebrous mansion all alone, save for the one insufficient servant (and now, me). He was a man who preferred his confidentiality and kept himself shut up in his apartment for an entire day, and who hired a private tutor ostensibly for his own edification at the price of one hundred pounds a year. That was the kind of person whose secrets were worth uncovering!

But I perceived that Mrs. Hawthorne would not be my accomplice any further that evening, so I politely excused myself to have an exploratory jaunt through the rest of the ground floor. I had to ignite a few lamps to aid my journey, as the waning natural light was not adequate for a true investigation of Bristlewood Manor, what with its innate dinginess.

I passed through the front parlor, which must not have entertained guests in years by the look of it. There I found nothing of note, as it appeared to be the standard of its type, if in need of a good dusting and some vivacity. And occupants. It was the same with the dining room, the breakfast parlor, the music room, and the billiard room, but the drawing room captivated my attention, if only because it seemed to double as a library. I stepped up to the shelves, which were loaded with books, and discerned the variety of the collection, which ranged from fiction of all kinds to history to science to religion to philosophy to etiquette. As a voracious reader, I figured this stock would keep me well-occupied during my free hours in the home.

On the wall across from the bookshelves, I spotted a pair of portraits hung in ovate wooden frames. The leftmost painting featured a handsome man of about fifty, with grayish-brown hair swept back from his face, piercing blue eyes beneath a wrinkled forehead, and a beard marking his jawline until it formed into a full mustache beneath a prodigious nose. The lady encircled in the other frame looked about ten years younger than the man and was comely like him; her dark brown hair fell in curled ringlets around her face, her nose was as petite as the fellow's was huge, and her green eyes sparkled like she knew something you did not, although it could have been nothing amusing.

A placard affixed to each frame revealed the couple to be Mr. William Fairfield and Mrs. Amelia Fairfield. The letter I had received had been signed by a Mr. H. Fairfield, so the Mr. Fairfield in the portrait could not be the same as the one who had hired me. I wondered, then, if these were his parents, and I attempted to blend their faces into one in my mind to picture what Mr. H. Fairfield might look like. Mr. William and Mrs. Amelia must have been dead if their son was now the master of Bristlewood Manor. If that were the case, how long ago had they perished? Had the home fallen into such disrepair when Mr. H. Fairfield took charge of it? If so, then why? And what kind of parents had they been if their son was now hiring a tutor for himself in adulthood?

These questions occupied my mind for some time as I continued to gaze upon the portraits. I wished the faces in the frames would speak to me, spilling the secrets of their family and their mansion. But not once did they move, neither to respire nor to blink; they simply stared off at something distant, well away from whoever had been painting them.

When it became painfully clear that Mr. William and Mrs. Amelia would offer me no information, I returned to the bookshelf and perused its contents until I happened upon a novel I had not yet taken up but had intended to read at some point. Ensconcing myself on one of the drawing room's sofas, I dove into it for the remainder of the evening, or, at least, until I began yawning incessantly. It seemed the inhabitants of the home did not take a late tea, which was all right by me; I hadn't the taste for it, although I had always feigned as if I did when necessary.

Outside, it was now full dark, and once my mind came back completely to where my body was, I could not shake the eerie sensation of being in Bristlewood Manor at night, no matter how stupid I told myself I was acting.

Taking in hand the oil lamp by which I had been reading, I got up from the drawing room to retire for the night. The rest of the ground floor was engulfed in shadows by then, with no hint of light anywhere, although I could not remember hearing Mrs. Hawthorne make her laborious journey up to the third-floor servants' quarters. As I advanced to the front stairs, it felt as if unseen eyes watched me go, and I once more chided myself for entertaining the thought.

I ascended the steps as noiselessly as I could, just in case my companions in the house were already in bed, and I took special care to dampen the sounds of my feet as I passed through the second-floor landing. I held my breath, too, but that was to mute myself for my own ears: I wanted to hear if anything was going on behind any of the closed doors of the master's apartment. Apprehending absolutely nothing, not even a snore, I continued upward.

The air in my room was much fresher now after having left the window open for several hours, a finding for which I was grateful upon entering. After shutting it, I quickly undressed and prepared myself for bed, hoping for a splendid night's rest so as to be in tip-top shape on the morrow when I finally met Mr. H. Fairfield.

But when I crawled under the covers, the inquiries I had asked of the portraits in the drawing room beleaguered my mind again. And though I was embarrassed by it, every little, inconsequential noise in the house made me start. No amount of self-scolding, it seemed, could despoil the inauspicious impression Bristlewood Manor had made upon me. Earlier in the day, the house's puzzles had thrilled me; however, now that I was alone in this bed, they rattled me.

I offered my prayers for protection and of thanksgiving to the Lord, and then I lay awake for at least an hour before sleep overcame me at last.

But it was only for a time.

# CHAPTER THREE

Something woke me abruptly.

In the initial confusion of being wrested from my sleep, it took me a moment to remember where I was and why I was there. I had no idea how long I had been passed out, but the thick darkness of the room around me indicated that dawn was still a long way off.

I freely admit to you, dear reader, that I was gripped by terror at that moment; and in a state of being so forcefully awakened, I hadn't the presence of mind to gather my wits about me. I did not know what had jarred me out of my slumber, but whatever it had been, it had left me in a cold sweat and trembling all over. That I was in a place like Bristlewood Manor did not help either.

And then I heard it.

It was a shrill, inhuman cry, issuing from who could say where. The sound pierced my nerves like an ice pick, forcing my shoulders to draw up tight to my ears and my chest to constrict.

Again feeling like I was not alone, I bolted upright in bed, my breaths coming in short, quick succession. My heart pounded so rapidly and violently that, in my paranoia, I feared it might crack my ribs.

I lit the candle on the bedside table, but the radiance of it didn't disclose any presence besides my own.

The shriek came again, this time more protracted and more tormented. It was not deafening, but it reverberated through the walls with a desperate fury, like something that would not abide going unheard, a distressed victim imploring me to witness its misery.

I cannot truly and completely convey to you the trepidation I felt, dear reader. The screams were like a confirmation of that foreboding I had endured throughout the day and, subsequently, had attempted to dispel as silliness. I had wanted to believe myself to be a logical, rational man, who was not predisposed and was willfully determined not to fall prey to the fantastical artifices of literature. But as a result of that, it seemed I had neglected to heed the omens of something awful about that house.

Pathetic as it may strike you, I whimpered like a child as I huddled in the bed, pressed into the corner of the room with my blankets drawn up to my chest. But tell me honestly: if you had heard those same things in a mansion as ostensibly sinister as Bristlewood Manor, would you have behaved any differently?

A long interval passed before I heard anything else, but when the horrific noise recommenced, it had changed. This time, it rang in as a consecution of identical wails, each clipped off at the end by the onset of the next.

"Ahh – ahh – ahh – ahh – ahh – ahh – ahh – ahh – ahh – ahh – ahh."

And on and on they went in what seemed like an interminable sequence, never altering or pausing even for a short breath.

The most ghastly images flashed before my mind's eye: depictions of torture, of vampires, of demons, of ghouls, of ghosts, of hellish creatures of which I had never even heard before. Which of those nightmarish scenes was playing out here in Bristlewood Manor? And why had I, of all the fools in the world, been so insufferably dense as to have accepted a post there?

The howls continued for an eternity, droning on until I nearly went mad with fright. But then, they suddenly stopped. All was abruptly and unsettlingly silent, save for the cudgel of my pulse and the crazed rhythm of my inhales and exhales.

I expected it all to start up again, but as the minutes passed and the quiescence persisted, I felt my body begin to relax. The whole episode could not have lasted more than five minutes from the time I had awakened. And yet, it had seemed as unending as my exacting vicar of a father had attested the agony of hellfire would be for the unrepentant.

I believed in the supernatural, of course. We all do at some level, especially in moments like that. And I believed that I had just had an irrefutable firsthand experience with it. Once I had reached a slightly calmer state of mind, I dismissed the more idiotic and ghastly possible explanations for what I had heard. But I could not convince myself that nothing at all had occurred. I was not a madman, and if I were, that would have been so much the better, because at least the hallucinations of a madman were not real. Whatever this had been, it was indubitably real.

And at that moment, what I perceived to be the most plausible rationale was that I had just heard the phantom cries of the late Mr. William Fairfield. Somehow, that seemed like an unassailable supposition, though the vociferations had not been particularly masculine nor feminine.

Was that a fatuous thought? Perhaps. Probably. But I am afraid you must read on to find out for yourself. I will not yet reveal the shocking account of the sounds.

I did not expect to re-enter the realm of slumber again that night, and, in fact, I sat up awake for quite some time. But the more I considered the ghost of Mr. William Fairfield, the less frightened I became and the more resolved to find answers I grew. Knowledge, I posited, was the opposite of fear, and I felt curiosity once again begin to overtake my anxiety. This did not necessarily have to be an unpleasant experience, frightening as it was at first; rather, it could end up being a gripping caper, and perhaps, the subject of an interesting book someday.

When I eventually got back to sleep, I slumbered until morning, but my dreams were, if you will allow the term, *outre*.

# CHAPTER FOUR

I arose with the gray dawn, instantly recalling what had transpired during the night. My first thought, however, was not one of dread; rather, I set an intention to ask Mrs. Hawthorne whether she had heard what I had, and if the sound was something perpetual. If she had been at Bristlewood Manor as long as she'd claimed, then she would likely be a treasure trove of useful information if I could wrench it out of her.

Standing up, I felt my night of poor sleep weigh heavily upon my body. However, I dressed as quickly – though still punctiliously – as I could and ran a perfunctory comb through my hair, eager to get downstairs and speak with Mrs. Hawthorne before Mr. Fairfield got up. I did not think, being a private man, the master of Bristlewood Manor would be particularly garrulous with respect to the mansion's more enigmatic and metaphysical qualities. And, while the housekeeper was a crotchety old crow, she had at least given me some information the previous day.

Mrs. Hawthorne was in the kitchen as she had been at suppertime yesterday, but this time, she was already seated at the table in the chair I had occupied at dinner, breaking her fast. She must have already delivered Mr. Fairfield his spread.

"Good morning, Mrs. Hawthorne!" I greeted her in as chipper a tone as I could manage.

She did not reply to me with words; instead, she simply pointed to the far opposite end of the table from her, where a small plate sat holding two poached eggs and a biscuit.

Assuming this had been set out for me, I settled down at that spot and began to eat. Apparently, she had not appreciated my sitting across from her the prior evening.

"It was very kind of you to make me breakfast this morning, Mrs. Hawthorne," I said, though it was certainly lackluster fare.

"Mr. Fairfield wishes that you do not starve," she replied with even less vigor than I thought possible. It seemed that her foul mood the day before was the rule rather than the exception. "Though why he is of that opinion, I cannot begin to guess."

The comment merely made me smile. There was something inexplicably attractive to me about an old curmudgeon like Mrs. Hawthorne. Somehow, I knew we would get along swimmingly. Or, at least, I would get along with her swimmingly. I had a premonition she might find herself wishing to feed me to a pack of wildebeests before our acquaintance met its end.

"Say, Mrs. Hawthorne," I began after taking a few more bites, "did you happen to hear anything strange in the middle of the night?"

Without looking at me or showing the slightest bit of interest in the question, she simply said, "No."

That was hard for me to believe since the screams had been quite loud up in my quarters. "Have you ever heard anything strange in the night here at Bristlewood Manor?"

"Never."

I found that claim even more difficult to accept. Even if there were nothing supernatural occurring in the mansion, and even if what I had experienced the night before had been an anomaly, one would have suspected that at least once in her time she would have heard something in the night that struck her as odd. But I decided not to challenge her on it because she seemed like one of those individuals who would dig in her heels just for the sake of doing so.

"I heard some very strange things last night myself," I told her instead. "It sounded like shrieking. It was like a ghost or something of that sort. And that made me wonder: Mrs. Hawthorne, is Bristlewood Manor haunted? It's not that I'm afraid of the place, you must know. In fact, I think the prospect is rather exhilarating."

She remained impassive and still hardly conscious of my presence. "What an absurd idea, Mr. Hayward," she said monotonously.

"Yes," I said with a forced laugh, "I suppose it must sound absurd. It could have been my fanciful imagination. But it seemed very real to me. I should say it was undeniably real."

"Perhaps Mr. Fairfield has hired a lunatic," she suggested.

"Perhaps he has," I chuckled. "I suppose that could be the case. Although, in all fairness, I have never been prone to lunacy before."

This time, Mrs. Hawthorne did flash a look in my direction. "Well, it is never too late to start," she said, almost portentously.

As bizarre as the statement was, I allowed it, since this was the most conversation I had gotten out of Mrs. Hawthorne thus far. Compared to how it all went yesterday, she was positively effusive this morning.

"Speaking of Mr. Fairfield," I said, "am I to meet him today? I am very much looking forward to making his acquaintance."

"Now, how am I supposed to know that?" she countered as if I was the most atrocious ignoramus she had ever met.

"Well, I thought that, perhaps, when he told you yesterday that he did not want to be bothered until this morning, he might have mentioned his plans for the day. Specifically, whether he intended to meet me."

"No," she said curtly.

"I see." I sat there quietly for a moment, thinking. Then I asked, "Mrs. Hawthorne, how long has Mr. Fairfield been the master of Bristlewood Manor?"

"I thought I told you yesterday I did not want any more of your questions," she snapped.

"Well, I do not mean to pettifog, madam, but I believe you said you had had enough of my questions for the now, and as it is currently a new now, I had surmised you might be willing to answer some more," I responded.

"You surmised incorrectly."

"Please, Mrs. Hawthorne, just give me a few answers and then I promise to leave you alone," I urged. "How long has Mr. Fairfield been the master of Bristlewood Manor?"

"Ever since he inherited it."

"And when was that?"

"After his parents were both dead."

I made myself grin good-naturedly at her. "Mrs. Hawthorne," I began, "I appreciate that you are giving me information that, for all intents and purposes, appears to be accurate. However, I should think you are well aware that your answers are not advancing my knowledge all that much."

"Oh, you noticed that, did you?" she said patronizingly.

"I did, indeed," I replied, tempering my frustration with her. I did not think she would deal well with being chastised, particularly by a comparative sapling like me. "I told you yesterday that I had no desire to be a nuisance to you, and that is still true. But I am afraid that, until I get out of you the intelligence I require, I shall have no other choice but to be a nuisance. And neither of us wants that, do we?"

She thought for a few seconds, biting her lip as she weighed her options. "You do not *require* anything, Mr. Hayward," she spat. "But if you *think* you *must* know, Mr. Fairfield's mother died some three and a half years ago, and his father died two years after she did. Mr. Fairfield moved in shortly thereafter."

"And where was Mr. Fairfield living before that?"

"That is quite enough for today," said Mrs. Hawthorne, getting up from the table.

"Please, Mrs. Hawthorne, I implore you," I cried, rising to my feet with her. "Just answer this one last question, and then I shall leave you be for the rest of the day."

She glared at me viciously, but she answered, "He was living in the West Indies."

"The West Indies!" I repeated. "What on earth was he doing there?"

Mrs. Hawthorne shook her head and held up her hand to me. "No more. You said that was the last question for today."

My need to know was so overwhelming that I was almost compelled to keep pressing her. But not wishing to compromise future investigations, I relented. "So I did, Mrs Hawthorne. So I did. Well, I thank you for your candor this morning. I hope you have an excellent day."

She merely grunted at me like she did not think that was a remote possibility and left the kitchen.

So. I'd had it confirmed to me that both Mr. William and Mrs. Amelia Fairfield were deceased, which aided me only insofar as I now knew they were both candidates for ghosthood. That Mr. H. Fairfield had not been living in England, had not even been living in Europe, at the time of their deaths was quite something, though. I just hungered to unearth what had taken him to the West Indies of all places.

After finishing my breakfast, I hunted down Mrs. Hawthorne again. This time, I only told her I would return to the drawing room to await Mr. Fairfield and asked her to inform him of that if he were to ask. She begrudgingly agreed, and I took my leave of her. In the drawing room, I took up my novel again until such a time as Mr. Fairfield deigned to introduce himself to me. My fascination with the man had augmented exponentially, and I was eager to meet him.

# CHAPTER FIVE

Mr. Fairfield finally appeared mid-morning. I was first alerted he would be coming downstairs presently when I heard his footsteps plodding on the ceiling above me. A few minutes later, his feet moved with a slow, heavy pace toward the stairs, and as he descended them, he sounded like an elderly, arthritic elephant.

Upon his reaching the bottom of the stairs, I perceived the voice of Mrs. Hawthorne saying, "Mr. Hayward is waiting for you in the drawing room, sir." Her tone was rich with all the respect for him that she had withheld from me.

"Thank you, Mrs. Hawthorne," said Mr. Fairfield. I had expected his voice to be deep and booming, something appropriate for the master of a large mansion, but instead, it was somewhat high-pitched for a man, grim, and barely audible.

I set aside my book and jumped to my feet, preparing to meet my pupil at last. But I was not at all ready for the sight of Mr. Fairfield when he entered the drawing room.

Reader, how am I to describe him to you? He was, at once, alluring and revolting. Allow me to further explain what I mean.

The first thing I noticed about him was his figure; he was tall but rail-thin, and the clothes he wore hung loosely from his body and had been put on sloppily. He was shockingly young, too, and I estimated he could have been no older than me, if not my exact age. His pale countenance, I admit, was dashingly handsome, with his father's vivid blue eyes and his mother's petite nose. However, he had a slovenly mien. His eyelids and under-eyes drooped as if he were not a proficient sleeper; his hair, which was dark brown and almost black like his mother's, had grown rather long, and it was unkempt and unwashed; as opposed to his father's well-groomed beard, his facial hair was patchy and stubbled, like he had merely forgotten to shave for some time instead of deliberately pursuing the fashion.

Mr. Fairfield was pallid, gaunt, and lugubrious. Nothing in his self-presentation was calculated to please, and yet he had a natural beauty that still shone forth, even if shaded by his personal negligence.

As I said: he was at once alluring and revolting. But the aspects I found revolting were those that could have been easily affected with a bit of care and attention.

"Mr. Hayward?" he asked by way of greeting. He stared searchingly at me with those bright eyes just as I was staring at him. And, though I had no good reason for it, I had an impression that he liked what he saw in me.

I bowed to him refinedly. "At your service, sir. It is a pleasure to finally make your acquaintance."

Mr. Fairfield returned the gesture, but stiffly and only with a slight dip of his head. "My name is Halifax Fairfield," he said in that alto voice. "I am the master of Bristlewood Manor. I thank you for accepting this post."

"It is a great honor to have accepted it, sir," I replied with an urbane smile. "When I received your letter in the post, I must admit that I was quite intrigued by the … unique nature of the offer."

"By the salary or by the lack of a child?" asked Mr. Fairfield. From anyone else, it might have been a jocular riposte, but from him, it was humdrum and dreary.

"I was intrigued by both, I must confess," I said, allowing myself a short chuckle.

But Mr. Fairfield did not chuckle or even smile back at me. He just continued to stand in the doorway of the drawing room; meanwhile, I remained on my feet in front of the sofa where I had previously been sitting. It was an awkward and cold exchange so far, the two of us posted so far apart from one another and not taking advantage of the numerous seating options available. It felt almost like we were facing off, or as if Mr. Fairfield wanted me to invite him to sit. But this was his house, and I would not presume to take the role of host.

"I am pleased to hear it," remarked Mr. Fairfield, though he sounded as if he had not experienced a feeling anywhere close to contentment in quite some time.

"If I may say, though, Mr. Fairfield, I am a bit confused as to what the nature of my work here is to be," I said, hoping I did not offend him with my questions. "If there is no child, are you to be my pupil then?"

"I am," he said simply. "Is that…" He paused, searching for a word before going on. "Is that amiable to you?"

"Yes, of course. It is quite amenable to me," I responded, slightly correcting his word choice, again intending no affront.

"Very good; then I should hope to begin right away," he said.

"Naturally, Mr. Fairfield." Then, no longer able to take this uncomfortable arrangement, I said, "Shall we have a seat, sir?"

Mr. Fairfield said nothing, but he silently trudged to the sofa across from mine, and we both sat down. He looked at me expectantly.

"Well, now," I began, unsure of what to say but recognizing that Mr. Fairfield either would not – or could not – take the lead, "as this is a unique situation, might I inquire as to what you hope to gain from my tutelage?"

Gazing blankly at the table between us now, Mr. Fairfield said, "I am hoping to gain very much. You see, I had a limited education as a child. In fact, my formal education ended when I was eight years old."

That stunned me. Mr. William and Mrs. Amelia Fairfield were certainly people of wealth and fine standing. Why would they not provide proper instruction for their son and heir beyond the age of eight?

But, outwardly, I acted as if this were a perfectly normal circumstance and said, "I see, sir. May I ask why that is?"

Mr. Fairfield looked at me … not sternly, as he appeared too feeble to be stern. But the look was enough of a change from morose to something approaching severe as to communicate sufficiently. "No, you may not," he replied.

Maintaining a calm demeanor, I said, "Of course, sir. I meant no offense. And I mean no offense when I ask the following: Do you know your letters?"

At that, Mr. Fairfield's ashen cheeks blushed bright red. "I can read and write at a basic level, but I have not had much use for the skill in recent years, so it has not been well practiced."

"Would you say, then, that reading and writing are a top priority for your education with me?" I asked.

"Yes, I would," he replied, still looking embarrassed by his nescience. "That and … how to present myself in society according to my station."

There could be no doubt as to Mr. Fairfield's need for assistance with regard to his outward aspect, although I found it curious to consider that his bedraggled condition might have been the result of ignorance rather than of laxity.

"Why, certainly, Mr. Fairfield," I acknowledged, still trying to convince him this was all so ordinary and there was no need for humiliation. It would be of no benefit to make him feel ashamed of himself, particularly not when he was motivated to improve.

"Where shall we begin?" asked Mr. Fairfield, and if I was not mistaken, I could have sworn I noted a hint, albeit a very faint one, of eagerness. All things considered, however, a faint hint of eagerness from Mr. Fairfield must have still been significant.

"Well, um, I say this once more intending no offense, Mr. Fairfield, but perhaps we ought to begin with a bath and a shave," I said, fearing the response that would get. I would not have worried about telling a boy under my tuition he needed to sharpen his hygiene, but it felt funny to do so when my student was also the master of the house.

But Mr. Fairfield merely nodded his understanding and acquiescence. "I admit I do not bathe as often as I should. It is such strenuous work for Mrs. Hawthorne to draw a bath, and I cannot be bothered to do it myself."

"Perhaps I could be of assistance in that respect," I offered, although that went far beyond the scope of a tutor's purview. "But why don't you employ more servants? There seems to be a need for them here."

"I do not desire to have them," said Mr. Fairfield simply. "I don't want a crowd of people in my house. I am content with few, and so I maintain few. My steward comes by once a week, and that is sufficient."

"But, sir, it is actually quite common for a man of your station to have many servants," I argued.

"I do not want them," repeated Mr. Fairfield.

"I understand, sir," I said, game to leave it at that. I was not about to argue with my employer in our first interaction. "Then, let us be on to the task."

After removing briefly to his apartment to procure clean clothes, Mr. Fairfield showed me to the ground-floor bathroom, which was thankfully near the kitchen, thus easing the acquisition of hot water. Once I had drawn him a bath that would be warm enough for his comfort, I gave him a bow and told him he could find me in the drawing room once he was finished.

"You are going to leave me alone?" he asked, sounding quite childish.

"Why, yes, of course, Mr. Fairfield," I said. "It would not do for me to not allow you your privacy."

"But I had servants to assist me in the bath when I was a boy," he replied. "Neither they nor I felt any bashfulness about it."

"Quite true, sir, but I am hired as your tutor, not as your valet," I reminded him. "It would be inappropriate for me to witness you in such a state. And it is, frankly, beyond any reasonable expectation for a tutor."

Mr. Fairfield looked despondent, or just more so than he typically did, but he said, "I suppose you're right. I shall meet you in the drawing room when I am through."

I bowed yet again and left the bathroom, mostly relieved at having escaped the situation.

You no doubt noticed the phrase "mostly relieved." And here, dear reader, is where I must reveal my secret, the one aforementioned in a couple of previous chapters. I assume you will not be scandalized by it, for you would not have gone to the effort of acquiring a book of this kind without having some of your own prurient interests.

I did not talk my way out of the bathroom because I would have been abashed to see Mr. Fairfield naked, but rather, because I had such a strong desire to see him naked. Ever since I was a boy, I had been fascinated with the nude male body, even before I knew anything about sexuality in general. I don't remember when it first started; it was something seemingly self-existent, always an indelible part of me. While I had two older brothers, I do not recall ever seeing them in a state of undress beyond their bare feet and legs in bedclothes. It must have been, I can only assume, the result of having my own body, for my interest had already been piqued long before I can recall ever seeing another male without any clothes.

From a young age, whenever I had the chance, I would marvel at my own nakedness, exploring the private parts I always hid beneath my clothes and about which I had been told so little; this obsession with myself only increased when I began to sprout new hairs down there and my apparatus grew to a manlier size. I discovered, at some point, that sometimes my penis would swell in thickness, length, and width, and if I touched it in the right way, particularly by rolling my foreskin back and forth, I could make myself feel so very good. At least, until the white stuff came out.

Anytime the white stuff came out, I always felt so very bad, so very ashamed of what I had done. However, while that shame was powerful, it was never enough to stop me from playing with myself another day, usually the next.

But it was not just my own nudity that tantalized me. I was likewise captivated by any works of art that featured men with fully exposed figures. Of course, I had to pretend as if I merely appreciated the artistry, when in reality, I cared for nothing of the sort so long as the subjects were males with bare bodies. It did not matter to me that they were fabrications; just the knowledge that someone had painstakingly drawn, sculpted, or painted that set of genitals was enough to exhilarate me.

Naturally, though, I preferred to see the real thing. On a few occasions during my adolescence, I happened to catch sight of some naked young men swimming (more on that later), which confirmed to me that the development of my suspended components was quite ordinary. At college, too, I had a handful of other opportunities to glimpse swinging penises, undulating scrotums, and jiggling buttocks. But there, the glimpses were always fleeting, for I could not afford to do anything other than peek. I never stared, and I certainly never touched, despite how very much I wished to do so.

That was because I knew this enchantment of mine was wicked and sinful, an unnatural and ghastly desire. The Crown hanged men from the gallows for acting on the same lusts I perpetually experienced, whether in my waking or sleeping. The fear of public shame, execution, and hell had all kept me in line, but they could not keep my eyes and thoughts from wandering.

And as you know, at times, when I was alone, my hands wandered too. It didn't take much to get me aroused, and when I did, I would partake of that most nasty act a man can do to himself, all the while recalling the images I had collected through the years. I was hopelessly addicted to touching myself down there, and I must assume you are too, if only so I can continue my tale without inhibition.

I thought Mr. Fairfield's unclad form must have made for a pretty sight. As disheveled and gloomy a man as he was, I could neither deny nor abate my decidedly carnal attraction to him. Even his hands, which had offered the only bare skin visible below the neck, were beautiful to me. The fingers were long and slender, quite feminine and delicate, and the nails were shapely, if in need of a trim and a scrub. Those hands were enough of a tease to whet my preoccupation with how the rest of his body looked beneath his clothes.

But I knew if I had stayed in the bathroom as he disrobed in front of me and sat naked in the tub, my eyes would have lingered on those special bits of flesh that so beguiled me, and there would have been no doubt of my animation by the unmistakable expression of it through my pants. I suppose at least some, if not most, of my readers will understand this; the rest of you, I fear, must find me quite vulgar.

I harshly reminded myself that I was at Bristlewood Manor to help Mr. Fairfield become a proper gentleman (and to earn one hundred pounds a year, lest I should forget), not to ogle the most intimate areas of his nude figure. I would not risk my reputation, life, and eternal salvation (and again, not to mention that one hundred pounds a year) to satisfy my iniquitous yearnings.

Would I?

No, of course not.

However, as I sat in the drawing room, attempting to read, my mind kept meandering off to the bathroom. It stirred me to know that at that very moment, he was completely nude, and try as I might, I could not stop imagining how fabulous Mr. Fairfield must have looked as he soaked in that tub, with every outward part of his body on full display. Instead of just enjoying the visualization, though, I found myself unexpectedly frustrated. Wrong as it was, there was simply nothing I loved more than the sight of a naked man. That was the plain and simple truth of the matter, although all of my exposure to such a delight had, to that point, been brief, forbidden peeps.

And yet, Mr. Fairfield had expressly requested I stay in there with him as he bathed, citing no shyness at the prospect of being seen in the nude. I was certainly not shy about seeing him in the nude but only about my reaction to it.

Oh, how I would have relished the opportunity to observe how he appeared without his billowing clothes! How I would have loved to measure the shape and size of his phallus, to investigate how much of the glans his foreskin covered, to see how low the warm water made his scrotum dangle, to follow the rounded cheeks of his posterior, to contrast the color of his nipples with that of his chest, to note if his toes were as long and slender as his fingers, to map out where his body had hair and where it was bare. I could have easily taken quick, furtive glances to add to the homoerotic gallery I kept stashed away in my memory. Moreover, it surely would have been simple enough to hide any evidence of my inevitable erection from him with a clever pose or even a towel.

But I was a damned coward and had begged off.

With exquisite fantasies of a naked Mr. Fairfield so completely occupying my mind, I could no longer focus on my book. My cock was already stiffening in my pants, and I readjusted myself so that it pointed upward, flat against my pubis, instead of jutting outward. I needed to get off this train of thought before Mr. Fairfield returned to the drawing room and caught me with a generous erection.

So I got up and went to the bookshelves to scan their titles again, this time with the assistance of daylight. Nothing I hadn't already seen the evening before caught my attention until I happened upon the spine of a thin, leatherbound book without anything imprinted on it. Intrigued for some reason, I carefully drew it off the shelf and unsealed its front cover. It was a diary, I found, the pages filled up with the same methodical, narrow calligraphy, quite different from the hand that had composed the job offer to me.

The entry on the first page was dated some five years back. I did not know to whom the journal belonged, or to whom it had belonged at one time, for there was no name inscribed on it. Although I figured it was the kind of breach of privacy against which I had been warned, I began to read the opening paragraph anyway:

*"We received word today from Robert that Halifax's marriage to Virginia has gone through. For any parent, this news should have produced so much joy, so much celebration, so much hope for*

*the future. But here in Bristlewood Manor, of course, there was nothing of the sort. I have grown so used to becoming somber the moment the name Halifax is mentioned, and I do whatever I can to avoid such moments if at all possible. It is like the proverbial 'slings and arrows' to react that way with respect to my only living child, but William prefers it as such. He behaves as if Halifax is not quite living, though not quite dead. Even upon such a marvelous occasion as this, my William could only offer a stiff nod and mutter the words 'very good' without the slightest touch of feeling. It felt as if he spoke merely of a fictional character I had grown fond of or a distant relative we never saw but for whom we, generally, wished the best. But I do not even think William wishes the best for Halifax; I think he only feigns interest for my benefit, though I am dubious he truly cares about my benefit at all. If it were up to him, he might as well not have a son."*

From the initial paragraph, I gleaned that this could only be Mrs. Amelia's diary. And what a fascinating detail right at the very beginning: Mr. Halifax Fairfield was married. That was ... unexpected. While any woman, I thought, would have been attracted to him, and certainly to his wealth, he did not carry himself in a manner that suggested he had a wife. Not to mention the fact that this was the first I was hearing of her existence.

I kept going, hoping to gain a clearer picture:

*"I wonder if we shall ever meet our new daughter-in-law. I wonder if we shall ever know our son as the man he is now. Knowing William's obstinacy better than anyone, I doubt it. But I fear my last concrete memory of Halifax will be the face of that terrified little boy we shipped off far away, the child we all but disowned to protect ourselves from the embarrassment of a crime I am now certain he could not have understood then. Oh, my dear*

*Halifax! Surely you have completed your penitence by now! But I dare not suggest such a thing to William. His shame and his wrath run deep. My only hope is that, with his marriage, Halifax will remain the heir to Bristlewood Manor. I cannot bear the thought of him spending the rest of his days on some remote island, even after his father and I are long gone. As of yet, I have not heard William speak of disowning Halifax completely, and I would never bring it up myself. But I live in constant terror that as we age, William will call upon his attorney to draw up a new – "*

I stopped reading when I heard footsteps approaching. Knowing them to be those of Mr. Fairfield, I quickly returned the journal to its place on the shelf and raced back to my seat, where I tried to compose myself and appear as if I had only been reading that novel the whole time my pupil was in the bath.

However, as I am certain you can imagine, my mind was in a tizzy, even more so than it was when I had been fantasizing about Mr. Fairfield in the tub. You must think I am fabricating this development, that the serendipity of so easily finding Mrs. Amelia Fairfield's journal – with the first entry devoted entirely to her son and my new master, no less! – is so absurd that it cannot be anything other than the convenient fluke only found in fiction. But I assure you, dear reader, this is exactly what happened. I cannot say whether some divine force guided me there by its omniscience and omnipotence; I can only report the solid facts of the matter, and I solemnly swear to have done so with the utmost fidelity to the truth. That it furthers and thickens the plot of my history is nothing but a wonderful coincidence.

When Mr. Fairfield entered the drawing room again, he still appeared tired and depressed, but the bath had brought a new buoyancy to his complexion, and the shave had made him appear altogether tolerable. His hair, though still wildly tossed about his head and in need of a trim, looked much better as well. The clean clothes he wore also fit him poorly, suggesting to me that the frailness of his figure was a more recently developed trait. But it was nothing a tailor could not remedy, and I was sure we would get around to that eventually.

All in all, he was now even more handsome to me than he had been before, and the craving to see him naked had become more acute. To keep my cock under control, though, I reminded myself that Mr. Fairfield was a husband. But that only made me wonder: where on earth was his wife? I was practically dying to find out, though, of course, I could not just blurt out the question, for then he would know I had been snooping. And besides, Mrs. Hawthorne had said on more than one occasion that he was a private man, and he had proven as much when he'd refused to tell me why his education had ended at age eight.

Although, now that I considered it, Mrs. Amelia Fairfield's journal entry had given me a small clue as to that, and it made me shudder to think of it.

"Do you feel like a new man now?" I asked, attempting to seem thoroughly innocent and jocose, like a fellow whose head was not flushed with questions and lurid mental pictures. "You certainly look like it."

"I do feel quite like a new man, good sir, and I thank you very much for the suggestion," he replied. I could not help thinking that, at times, he sounded overly and clumsily formal, as if he understood the importance of gentility but not its proper implementation. He crossed the room and regained his seat on the sofa across from me. "What is the next task, Mr. Hayward?"

"Well," I said, suddenly realizing I had given no forethought to the course our business together ought to take, "it would be a great help to me if I were to have a better understanding of the areas where you need – er, where you would like to see growth."

"I have already explained that to you, Mr. Hayward," muttered Mr. Fairfield, looking annoyed, his cloddish punctiliousness having briefly dissipated. "Letters and those matters appropriate to my station."

"Quite right, and so you did," I acknowledged. I supposed that would be enough to work with until I had more time to set us a solid plan. "Well, the first step in solving any problem is gaining a proper understanding of its nature. As such, I would like to begin by analyzing your level of comfort with reading. You have said your ability is basic, and it would help me a great deal to know just how basic it is. Do you have any paper we could use?"

Without a word, Mr. Fairfield got up and went over to a desk in the corner. From its drawer, he brought out some blank pages, and from its otherwise desolate surface, a quill pen. He came back, handed them to me, and returned to his seat.

"Thank you, sir," I said with an appreciative nod. Still improvising, I picked up the novel I had been skimming, a beloved love story published some years back. I did not know if it would be of any interest to Mr. Fairfield, but I wanted to appear as if I had some sort of premeditated method; I was supposed to be a professional, after all. "I would like you to read aloud from this book, and as you do, I will note the words with which you struggle. Do you mind if I come and sit beside you so that I might look over your shoulder at the text?"

"Not at all," said Mr. Fairfield with a shake of his head. He patted the seat next to him invitingly.

I stood up and crossed the room to him. He was sitting directly in the middle of the sofa, and he did not move over with my approach. Very well, then. I settled myself on his left. Our bodies were so close to one another that I could feel his heat, and, wryly, I mused to myself how thankful I was that I had made him wash off his odors as the first order of business. But our proximity unnerved me, given my earlier reveries about him. We did not touch, but being so near him was exhilarating and distressing at the same time.

Sufficiently maintaining my outward composure, however, I handed him the book and set my paper and pen on the table in front of us. "Now, go ahead and read aloud," I instructed him. "Don't concern yourself with impressing me. I am not here to be impressed but to assist, and I can only assist if I have precise insight into the ways in which you require assistance."

With a nod, Mr. Fairfield opened the novel to page one. It took him a while, but he managed to make out the first sentence: "It is a truth universally acknowledged, that a single man in possession of a good fortune, must be in want of a wife."

"What a daffy claim," he scoffed in response to it.

Well, that was certainly a strange take on the line, especially from a married man! It required some exertion not to pursue it any further, although it certainly seemed like an invitation to ask about his marital state.

But instead of that, I said, "Well, the novel is fiction, so it is well within the constraints of its genre. Keep reading."

He did, reciting the book's contents to the best of his ability. And indeed, I discovered right away that his reading skills were quite rudimentary. Having had some learning as a boy, many simple words he knew by sight and others he could reasonably sound out; however, I was still surprised by the sheer number of terms that were lost on him completely. It saddened me that a man of his looks and inheritance should find himself in such dire straits, though I took some comfort in his motivation not to remain as he was in his impaired education.

And yet, I could reasonably attribute his lack of instruction to being cast off from his family at a young age, though for what reason, I still did not know. For some unspecified "crime," his mother had written. But what crime could a child so young have perpetrated to require such a brutal consequence? I felt a knot form in the pit of my stomach as I listened to this beautiful young man struggle so mightily with the written language, knowing, as I did but minimally, the hardship he must have endured in his life. Whatever his quirks and peculiar habits, I was determined to help him rise out of the pit into which his parents had, apparently, so mercilessly thrown him.

If only I could have forecast then how that objective would utterly ruin me. But now I seem to be getting ahead of myself, and this chapter has run on far too long.

# CHAPTER SIX

We spent a significant fraction of the day slogging through the initial chapter of that novel, and by the time Mr. Fairfield had reached its end, I'd made an extensive tabulation of words that had bedeviled him. Going through the list together, I aided him in sounding out each word on its own; then we found them one by one in the book's text, and I told him to reread the full sentence from whence it had come to help him grow accustomed to the word before his eyes and on his tongue. After explaining the definitions of the trickier ones, we discussed their use in the context of the story.

For being entirely improvised, I was quite pleased with the first lesson I gave in my private tutoring career. It was challenging for him without being laborious or impossible, and it was relevant to my pupil's needs. I doubted I could have created anything significantly better if I had invested two hours' worth of planning into it.

I must confess there were a few moments when my eyes wandered. With Mr. Fairfield immersed in the book, I had the opportunity to glance over at his lap, though I was thwarted in my effort to discern any details by the thickness of the fabric. It was wholly inappropriate, of course, and I asked God to forgive my indiscretion, but I was enamored. It floored me to think I was close enough to reach out my hand and clutch him, though naturally, I would never have dared to do so.

Around noon, I asked Mr. Fairfield if he was not quite ready for lunch, but he informed me he only took one meal a day, and that meal was the one Mrs. Hawthorne left outside his door every evening. Deciding that a lesson on the importance of eating regular meals was better left for another day and that I was not particularly hungry myself, I continued on with him until evening. At that point, Mr. Fairfield thanked me for my time and said he had rather enjoyed himself. Then he retired to his apartment, explaining he preferred to dine alone upstairs.

With a satisfied smile, I noticed he took the novel with him, perhaps to re-read the first chapter with his new knowledge. That was quite endearing to me, and his enthusiasm promised great future success.

By the time Mr. Fairfield left me, I was half-starved, so I went into the kitchen to see what Mrs. Hawthorne had made. Again, I found she was putting together a tray for the master, and I made up a plate of food for myself. When she returned from delivering it to him, we sat once more at opposite ends of the table to eat our suppers.

But I could not just leave her in peace. It was not that I wanted to pester her for the sake of it; I simply did not like the lack of conversation. And besides, I had more questions for her.

"How was your day, Mrs. Hawthorne?" I asked jovially.

"The same as any other, I suppose, but now with an annoying interlocutor to frustrate my pleasantly silent meals," she replied in her usual manner.

I grinned at her. "I understand that changes to routine can be quite difficult at first, but is my presence so utterly irritating to you?"

"It is," she said.

"My most earnest apologies then," I said, stifling a giggle. "I hope that, in time, I will begin to grow on you."

"You are already beginning to grow on me. Like a pox."

"Oh, my dear Mrs. Hawthorne," I laughed aloud, appreciating her turn of phrase, "you are such a hoot."

She actually winced at the compliment but did not respond to it. Even that was charming in its own way.

"Do you expect Mr. Fairfield to return to us from his apartment this evening?" I asked.

"Once he goes up, he stays up," she said.

"I see." Then, hoping she had forgotten my promise not to lavish her with more questions the rest of the day, I asked, "Mrs. Hawthorne, would you mind if I asked you how Mr. William and Mrs. Amelia Fairfield died?"

Mrs. Hawthorne groaned at me and rolled her eyes. "Who taught you that such things were appropriate for dinner conversation?"

"I am afraid my family was at our most morbid when we were at the table as I was growing up," I lied. "I hope you will indulge me with just a touch of nostalgia for home."

Mrs. Hawthorne looked me square in the eye. "Mrs. Amelia hanged herself from a second-floor window. Mr. William succumbed to consumption two years later. Are you quite satisfied now?"

She said it all as if trying to shock me out of my curiosity.

"Erm, yes, I am, thank you," I replied. I had not expected that detail about Mr. Fairfield's mother, and it rather ruffled me. And then, for the first time since I had met Mr. Fairfield that morning, I remembered the haunting noises I'd heard in the night and the postulation I'd made that they had come from ghosts.

I allowed Mrs. Hawthorne to finish her meal in peace then. For now, I had much to consider and a desire to get done eating so I might return to Mrs. Amelia Fairfield's journal in search of more answers.

When I went back into the drawing room, I slid the diary from the shelf where I had left it and slipped it into my waistcoat before going up to my quarters. I would have preferred to do my reading downstairs, but considering the sensitive material, I figured it would be far better to have my privacy.

After changing into my nightclothes, saying my prayers, and lying down on the bed, I crossed my legs at the ankles and picked up where I had stopped reading earlier:

*"– will so that he might name someone else, someone he believes is more worthy, as his heir. His faults may be what they may be, but my Halifax does not deserve this unending punishment. It has been more than ten years since that bitter day, for God's sake! Now, he has a wife, and surely that must be proof of his reformation! But I am afraid to mention it to my husband. I am afraid to mention to him anything with a tangential relationship to that awful thing young Halifax did as a boy, lest I remind William so much of his anger that he acts with even more vindictiveness. William put so much hope upon Halifax when he was born, for he was the only one of our children to survive. I believe he was so heartbroken by Halifax's waywardness that he resolved that forgiveness in life was impossible. It is a torment to me, and my only hope is that William's fury does not extend beyond his death."*

There, the entry ended. As I flipped through the next several pages, I saw that Mrs. Amelia had only taken up her diary periodically, sometimes with weeks and sometimes with months passing between periods of writing. Other than that first episode, she narrated her life as if she did not have a son at all, detailing instead the various goings-on of her social circle as well as her frustrations with the service staff (of which, at that time, it seemed Bristlewood Manor had many).

Perhaps she, too, had wished to forget about her child on occasion.

I followed Mrs. Amelia through a year and a half of her intermittent chronicle when I, at last, came upon another account related to her son.

*"A letter came in the post today from Richard,"* wrote Mrs. Amelia Fairfield, *"announcing that Halifax and Virginia had welcomed a child, a daughter named Sophie, into the world. Just think! I am now a grandmother. But, alas, as always, I cannot take any joy in the news. For, just as expected, when I shared it with William, he was as impassive as ever, if not more so. That insolent man! I dare say I now regret that I ever married him, that I ever bore his child, even that I was ever born. For indeed, it now seems as if Halifax truly is not our child anymore. He never writes, nor does he include any greeting in Richard's letters. These missives from Antigua may as well be fictional concoctions of Richard's for as much interaction with their characters as I receive!*

*"But if Halifax resents us, I cannot blame him in the slightest degree. His father is a bitter, cruel man, who seems to survive only on the hatred he feels for his own son. That loathing has not been abated by Halifax's growth into manhood, nor by his marriage, nor, now, by the birth of his daughter. If anything, time has only allowed William's grudge to further blossom. William actually had the temerity to ask why he should care when I told him about Sophie's birth! When I expressed it in terms of us now being grandparents, he dismissed it, saying that, no, we were not! He*

*went even further, and tears now fall from my eyes as I write this: 'We are not to acknowledge that boy's existence any longer,' he declared. 'I never want to hear his name pass your lips again, nor for you to make any oblique reference to him. He is a stranger in a far-off land, and we will treat him as such.' But what, I asked, of our granddaughter? 'She is nothing to us,' he said. 'Just another stranger in a far-off land. The squalling brat of a squalling brat.' Then, I let loose upon him, unleashing every word of contempt I had kept inside for years. I raged and raged, and I only quit when he struck me across the face, knocking me to the ground. With tears in my eyes, I told him I never wanted to see him again, and he reciprocated the sentiment.*

*"But I cannot just leave him. I have nowhere to go, no money besides what I have from him, no living family of my own. I am trapped in Bristlewood Manor, this godforsaken, wretched, suffocating place of misery. If there is a hell on earth, it must be here. I hate my life. I hate myself. I hate the world. The only love I have is for Halifax, and we are separated by an ocean, and I cannot reach him. That love may as well not exist either. I have become despair itself, and I cannot live another day. I will not."*

I turned the page, but the next leaf was blank. In fact, there was no more writing in the book at all after that.

Flipping back to the beginning of the final entry, I beheld the date: Mrs. Amelia had scrawled this entry three and a half years ago. And according to Mrs. Hawthorne, that was when she had died, having killed herself by hanging from one of the house's second-story windows.

Gooseflesh spread over my entire body, and tears welled up in my eyes as I contemplated the tragedy that had beset Bristlewood Manor. A young child sent away for some unknown misdeed. A father consumed by such enmity that he would not relent in his unforgiveness. A mother so vanquished by grief that she took her own life.

It was all so horrid, so gut-wrenching, so unimaginable. And I had stepped right into it. Well, to be fair, I was sticking my nose into it; I could have gone about my business as a tutor without needing to know the whole backstory. However, as I was naturally curious, and as I had heard those terrible noises in the night, I thought I could be forgiven for my nosiness.

But what could have been young Mr. Halifax Fairfield's sin? I could not fathom anything a child could do that would have been so grievous that he must be exiled across the sea for the remainder of both of his parents' days.

I reread Mrs. Amelia's final written testimony, and only then did I recall the catalyst for the conflict between her and Mr. William. Mr. Halifax was not only a married man; he was a father too! Where were my pupil's wife and daughter?

Mrs. Amelia's diary had given me great insight into Mr. Halifax Fairfield's background, but it had also seeded new, disconcerting questions. I very much doubted I would stumble upon another journal to answer them, but Mr. Fairfield and, surely, Mrs. Hawthorne had the information I sought. The only uncertainty was how I could extract it from them.

# CHAPTER SEVEN

The screaming began anew and brought me at once out of my hard-won sleep. The first thought to enter my mind was that these must be the howls of Mrs. Amelia's – rather than Mr. William's – tortured ghost. I believed such things were possible, particularly in places where considerable tragedy and horrible deaths had occurred. And if any place was ideal for a haunting, it seemed that it would be Bristlewood Manor. Mrs. Amelia herself had christened the house a "hell on earth."

"Ahh – ahh – ahh – ahh – ahh – ahh – ahh – ahh – ahh – ahh – ahh."

The wailing was, in every respect, identical to the way it had sounded the previous night, at least after it had transmogrified into that nasty series of wild yelps.

While I was, again, terrified, I could not just lay there helplessly in bed until the cries finally ended. There was too much mystery and intrigue at Bristlewood Manor for that.

Pushing away the covers, I swung out my legs and planted my bare feet on the floor. I reached for the candle on the bedside table and lit it. Then, standing up, I turned toward the door.

I nearly dropped the candle in alarm at what I saw.

The door to my room was standing wide open.

That was not how I had left it. I knew without the tiniest morsel of doubt that I had shut the door tightly before I went to sleep. I'd wanted the utmost privacy while reading Mrs. Amelia's journal, and I would never have slept with the door open anyway.

I twirled back around to look at the bedside table.

The diary was gone.

I checked the floor and the top of the tallboy, just in case I had set it elsewhere without remembering. But it was nowhere to be found.

My breaths came in short rasps. I had not heard anyone enter my room during the night, but I felt sure I would have. I had always been a light sleeper, prone to waking up at the slightest provocations. However, there could be no doubt that *something* had been in here. I write *something*, dear reader, because, at that moment, I was open to the possibility of the intruder being non-human. Or, at least, not entirely human. Or not at all human … anymore.

The ghastly sounds continued as I stood there, paralyzed by this bone-chilling fright. The blood raced through my body at a frantic pace, and I felt the need to act. But what could I do? No thought would come to me; or rather, no useful thought would come to me. I was now convinced a spectral soul dwelled in this house, and I could not conceive of anything in my power to do about it. All I wanted was for the shrieking to stop and to know who (or what) had been in my room while I was sleeping.

My impotence in that situation deeply distressed me. What is one to do in the face of such insuperable dreadfulness? Helplessness must be one of the worst human experiences, and I felt absolutely helpless.

But I was resolute in the need to do something. Anything. I hadn't had a plan that morning when I began tutoring Mr. Fairfield, and that had gone off profitably. So, trusting my ability to extemporize, I slipped out of my small bedroom, still clutching the candle in my trembling hand.

Once I was out in the corridor, I could perceive that the menacing racket was not ubiquitous; rather, it had a definite source, and it came from below me. Rising up onto the balls of my feet to muffle my steps, I issued toward the stairs, down which I went meticulously. I did not know if phantoms were pansophical and thus couldn't be snuck up on, but if they weren't, I wanted to avoid alerting this entity to my approach.

Upon reaching the second floor, a lump formed in my throat as I pinpointed this to be the origin of the yowling. Mrs. Hawthorne had admonished me in the clearest terms that I was never to spend any time on this level beyond what it took to pass through it on my way to my quarters. However, my spooked curiosity impelled me to advance against my better judgment. I left the candle on the landing to provide a minute bit of light by which to see without completely flaunting my presence.

Into that forbidden passageway I went, passing closed doors as I followed the ghoulish din. It was an effort to keep my breath steady and even. My entire body quaked with intense agitation. My blood pulsated in my ears. I hadn't the slightest idea of what I would do when I came upon the thing persisting in this hideous clamor, but that did not preclude my compulsion to probe its nature.

The radiance of the candle had nearly ceased to be of any assistance by the time I reached the door of consequence. It was indisputable: the cacophony emanated from the chamber behind it. The bedlam was so much louder now than it had been in my room, so inordinately sonorous that it ground my nerves like a grain mill.

After pausing to bolster my mettle, I placed a tremulant hand on the knob, twisted it tenderly, and silently pushed on the door, opening it just a few centimeters.

There, I beheld a most astounding sight. Prepare yourself, dear reader. I don't know what you expect, but I couldn't have predicted the reality if I'd been given a thousand guesses.

In an otherwise empty room, illuminated only by the pale light of the moon and a pair of candles placed on the floor at his feet, Mr. Fairfield sat in a chair with his back to me and a full-length mirror set up in front of him. In the reflection, I saw that he was completely naked, that his penis was conspicuously erect, and that he was vigorously masturbating. All the while, he wailed and gaped at himself in the mirror like a bawdy Narcissus.

The cries, I now understood, were not the ghostly shrieks of pain and agony, but the quintessentially human squalls of sexual ecstasy.

Dear reader, I wish I could tell you I left Mr. Fairfield to carry out this most intimate activity in privacy, that I accepted it was his business and his alone, no matter how distasteful it may be. But that would not be the truth. You might not be surprised at that, given what you now know about me and my druthers.

I stood there in the hallway with my face pressed into the small aperture I had created, transfixed by this almost unbelievable exhibition.

The light was dim, so I could not observe much in the way of fine detail, but what I could discern was sufficient to enchant me. Mr. Fairfield's nude body was, as I had suspected, stunningly beautiful, unimpeachably appetizing.

Despite the emaciation caused by his habit of skipping meals, his limbs were stalwart with muscle. His skin, though so white it almost glowed, was smooth and sleek, interrupted only by a copse of brown pubic hair and his two brown nipples, which were each three-quarters of an inch in diameter. The sweat of his effort left him luminous in the faint light, somewhat resembling an angel of sorts. I certainly found him angelic, despite the hellish commotion he expelled.

And now for the most important part, the writing of which will no doubt heat me up even now: from what I could see of his cock between the rapid up-and-down motions of his right hand, it was neither large nor small, neither too thick nor too thin, but perfectly average in size, precisely the way I preferred it. With a name like Halifax Fairfield, I surmised he must have had a foreskin, although I could not clearly observe it in the dark. His scrotum, which was mostly submerged in shadow, jostled with each swipe of his hand.

You might assume that I, too, had grown rather stiff beneath my nightclothes as a result of this, and in that, your assumption would be correct. I had never before witnessed another man pleasuring himself and had often believed I must have surely been the only one who did it. To say that this splendor entranced me would be an egregious understatement. Every thought vanished from my consciousness, the fear I had felt just moments before now erased by this new, heretofore unimaginable circumstance. I was watching another man – and not just any other man, but my employer, my student, and the master of Bristlewood Manor – sit without a shred of clothing and rabidly stimulate his phallus while regarding it all — and exposing it all to me — in a mirror.

That last element of the scene as I just described it particularly intrigued me then. It was plainly evident that Mr. Fairfield enjoyed the sight of himself tossing off in the nude like that, and the candles had obviously been arranged in such a way as to accentuate his verboten regions. I remembered back to the days when I, too, had enjoyed examining the reflection of my nakedness and stroking myself toward the mirror, yearning for the chance to scrutinize another man in the same way. Could that possibly mean Mr. Fairfield was like me? Was he titillated by all male bodies or only by his own? When he'd asked me to stay in the bathroom with him while he stripped down and bathed, had that been specifically because he wanted me to see him in the raw? Might he have asked me to disrobe and join him in the tub? Would his cock have become wooden at the sight of me as mine would have become at the sight of him? Would we have touched each other's bodies, exploring all of those taboo constituents, until we muddled the bathwater with our spendings?

I don't know what madness gripped me then, but I must expect I am not alone in behaving irrationally when overcome by prurient exigencies. Do not lie to yourself, dear reader; if you have made it this far in the book, you must certainly have done outlandish things in fulfillment of your lusts!

As if driven by an irresistible, unseen force, I found myself pulling up my nightclothes until my exorbitantly firm penis met the open air. Tucking the clothes under my chin, I wrapped my fingers around the familiar shape of my erection and tugged on it in my particular way, sliding the foreskin back and forth over the head with the same pace and rhythm as Mr. Fairfield kept in his self-stimulation. I'd only ever masturbated to mental images or my own reflection prior to that, and doing so now, with someone to watch, someone I found so attractive, brought me an almost unreal sensation of ecstasy.

However, the few minutes I'd already stood gaping at him had aroused me so much that, by the time I finally touched myself, my orgasm did not tarry long in arriving. Within two minutes, I attained the point of inevitability at which climax becomes assured. My muscles tensed up, my chest rocketed forward, and a moan escaped my lips as thick ropes of semen spewed forth from my cock, coating the door and the floor with their viscidity.

# CHAPTER EIGHT

Only once in my life before that night had I been caught with my prick in my hand. I must have been fourteen or fifteen years old then, and it had been one of those occasions (to which I have previously referred) when I'd chanced upon a small group of military men, who had been stationed briefly in our area, nude-bathing in the river. The oldest could not have been more than ten years my senior, but I saw them all as mature, grown men, complete with dark body hair and full-formed, swaying penises. Hidden from their sight, I was transfixed by the theater, monitoring it and rubbing myself through my trousers until they got dressed again. Then, I raced home, suddenly remembering I had left some responsibility or other incomplete.

But during my journey, a thirst for physical relief so mightily prevailed upon me that I stole into one of Mr. Rochester's barns, which was presently unoccupied. Unable to endure it any longer, I frantically pushed down my trousers to free my hoisted, leaking cock, the foreskin of which had already receded. Grabbing it in my hand, I desperately thrashed my prick as I closed my eyes and brought to mind the naked soldiers, needing to finish up quickly so as to get back to the vicarage. I could feel myself getting close when I heard someone clear their throat.

My eyelids flipped open, and standing there was Mr. Greene, Mr. Rochester's bailiff. He gawked at me, looking quite embarrassed at finding me like that.

But if he was embarrassed, I was mortified; not only was I on full display, but I was aroused and taking advantage of it.

My breath catching in my throat, I released my penis, squatted down to grab my trousers, and ripped them up to my waist, concealing myself again. My face burned with shame, and I felt as if Mr. Greene might snatch me by the ear and drag me before Mr. Rochester. Or worse, before my father.

"Best not make a habit of that, son," he said calmly and with a nod. "It will lead you down a bad, bad road, one unfit for any decent man, much less the son of a vicar."

"I'm sorry," was all I could think to say. What else could I say, anyway?

"It is not me you should be saying sorry to," he replied, "but to your God and to your future wife."

The thought of a woman getting anywhere close to my cock made me shudder. "You won't tell my father, will you?" I rasped.

"Oh, heavens, no," said Mr. Greene, waving a hand as if to dispel my fear (which it didn't do). "You are a boy, and that is what boys do, whether we like to admit it or not. But I will just tell you, it is an unseemly bit of business to be about. That part of you was made for procreation, not for recreation. And whatever lady you were picturing with your eyes closed like that, she is another man's future wife. Or maybe another man's current wife. I don't know. But it is quite wrong for you to treat a woman and her man like that. I'm certain you do not need me to cite the Lord's words on that matter."

"No, sir," I said, knowing all too well the biblical passage to which he referred. I appreciated that he had normalized, somewhat, the practice of masturbation, but I felt immense shame at the fact that I had not been picturing a woman at all, married or not. If tossing off to thoughts of a woman was sinful, how much worse was it to toss off to thoughts of a whole group of naked military men?

"Now, get on out of here," said Mr. Greene with a crick of his neck. "And mind you keep your hands where they belong."

I sprinted home with my prick now flaccid if yet unsatisfied. I had never felt so compunctious, never felt so humiliated.

Not until I ejaculated in the hallway of Mr. Fairfield's apartment, that is.

Immediately, I understood the gravity of my lapse in judgment. Mr. Fairfield had overheard the sound I'd made and, before I could step back into the corridor, he whipped his head around toward the door. I sprinted toward the stairs with my softening cock whipping against my thighs, heedless of the clatter of my feet pounding on the floor and neglecting to retrieve the candle from the landing.

With any luck, I thought, the darkness and the narrowness of the breach in the doorway had obscured my identity from him. But, in reality, I knew it would not be difficult for Mr. Fairfield to ascertain who the voyeur had been. Mrs. Hawthorne could not have moved as swiftly as I had in my flight, and I doubted she'd ever let out such an orgasmic shriek in her life.

And she certainly could not have left that unmistakable seminal fluid on the door and the floor.

My time at Bristlewood Manor was surely at an end, almost before it had even begun. The only question was whether it would conclude momentarily or linger on until morning.

My racing feet carried me through the darkness back to my room on the third floor. And once inside my quarters again, I was reminded of the other peculiar elements of this exceptional night: the open door and the bereft bedside table.

What I had attended in Mr. Fairfield's apartment now promoted a new conjecture: Could Mr. Fairfield have invaded upon my privacy as I had invaded upon his? Was it he who had swiped the journal and left my door wide open?

The notion seemed preposterous and a touch arrogant to me. Why should he have cared to spy on me? However, my examination had led me to the conclusion that the noises, which had now ceased, were not otherworldly in essence, so the possibility of a ghost having entered the room seemed unlikely. Furthermore, having failed to hear Mrs. Hawthorne ascend to the third floor a second night in a row, I had concluded that she must have kept her quarters on the ground level because of the strain of climbing the stairs. Therefore, it must not have been her.

In that case, it could have only been Mr. Fairfield!

That is, unless there were other people in the house of whose presence I was not aware.

I had to physically suppress the resurgence of my dinner at that idea, but I could not suppress the misgivings it precipitated. My mind rushed right away to Virginia and Sophie, Mr. Fairfield's wife and daughter, whose whereabouts were still unknown to me. Had he brought them back to England from the West Indies and locked them away somewhere as prisoners in this house? And, if so, did one or both of them avail themselves of his nocturnal self-indulgence to peregrinate through the mansion?

No possible explanation could assuage the revulsion I felt as I sat on my bed, hidden behind a closed door again. Perhaps it would be better for me to be expelled from Bristlewood Manor after all, I thought. The only point on which I waffled was whether I should not just abscond right then, in the middle of the night, before I had to face Mr. Fairfield again.

You must be thinking this would have been the only sensible course of action, and, therefore, I suppose you must be left quite perplexed now when I tell you I did not quit Bristlewood Manor that night. I had a few justifications for this, and I pray you will acquit the less noble of the list. I shall only lay them out bluntly and without apologia: there were the one hundred pounds per year; there was the allure of what I had caught Mr. Fairfield doing and the pulchritude of his naked body; there was the thirst to fully unravel the mysteries of Bristlewood Manor; and there was the commitment I had made to help Mr. Fairfield complete his education.

Feeling a sudden chill come over me, I crawled back under the covers, though I did not lay down to sleep. I kept expecting Mr. Fairfield to turn up in my room at any moment, cast into a blind rage at me for having trespassed in his apartment, for having encroached upon his licentious avocation, for having deposited my seed so haphazardly, for having pilfered and studied his mother's diary.

But nothing of the sort took place. I did not hear so much as a footstep from down below. I almost wished for something to happen; waiting without knowing was torturous. What thoughts were passing through Mr. Fairfield's mind at that moment? It was impossible that he shouldn't know he'd been detected, but did he know for a fact it had been me? And if so, what was his reaction to it? Was he scandalized or was he intrigued?

The former was, of course, the most likely, but the latter petrified me. Allow me to attempt an explanation, because I should think some of my readers may not comprehend this implicitly.

If Mr. Fairfield were to have been intrigued by my spying on him in that state of bald-faced masturbation, then it seemed possible he might have desired me to join him in his exploits. You know already this would have been profoundly seductive to me, and yet, you also already know I believed in my bones that capitulating to such carnal lusts would have been a sin of the most depraved sort. Two things can be true at once: in this case, attraction and repulsion, just as I had experienced on first beholding Mr. Fairfield earlier that day.

In the immediate aftermath of my recklessness, I felt colossal guilt for having lasciviously surveilled my employer and condescended to my baser instincts. If Mr. Fairfield had, somehow, failed to see me, I knew God had. There may not have been a spectral presence haunting Bristlewood Manor, but that didn't mean I wasn't haunted by supernatural fears. Visions of hell alternated with wistful remembrances of Mr. Fairfield's nude body and grim projections of my next interaction with him.

But, invariably, after a half-hour or so, the remorse subsided somewhat, overpowered again by lust. We are so very quick to forget, and we rarely make the same mistake only once. I'd never understood how that could happen. However, all my life, I had existed in that capricious cycle of regret followed by eventual arousal followed by masturbation followed by orgasm followed by fresh regret. I could even toss off while being fully aware that as soon as I finished, I would sink into a pit of self-loathing.

And so, at some point, the mental picture of a naked Mr. Fairfield completely overtook my awareness, and my penis stirred underneath my clothes. In spite of everything, I was incapable of resisting its call.

I threw off the covers, stripped off my nightshirt, and threw it onto the floor. I'd always been fain to masturbate naked when possible. Taking my cock in my left hand, I began to graze its sensitive surface. Meanwhile, the fingers of my right hand gently pet my balls, coaxing along their production.

On the grand stage of my mind, a new scene debuted. In it, I threw open the door to Mr. Fairfield's room and marched right up to him, interpolating myself between his chair and the mirror. As he gaped at me in shock, I shed my bedclothes, unveiling my imposing pillar before his wide eyes.

However, this fantasy did not go any further than that. At the very moment I imagined myself showing him my stiff prick, my toes curled up in my third-floor bedroom, and I blew a cascade of sperm all over myself.

I presume it bears no exposition as to what I felt as soon as the first drop fell onto my belly, so I will not dredge up that well-worn subject again.

Sleep did not easily return to me the rest of that night, and when it did, it was only because my exhaustion had so exceeded my perturbation that I could not avoid dozing off.

As I slept, I dreamed about sucking Mr. Fairfield's cock.

# CHAPTER NINE

Morning came, and I awoke in misery. My eyes stung and my head throbbed from another night of so little sleep, and my muscles and joints ached from being clenched in fear. Moreover, the awareness that I would soon have to face Mr. Fairfield was a further mental agitation that only exacerbated the affliction I felt in my body.

It did not help that I was still naked and had a prominent erection upon regaining consciousness.

Consequently, I had no appetite to speak of, so I allowed myself to stay in bed for a while longer, fretting over everything I could think to fret over until such a time as it became necessary for me to get up.

This time, I managed to avoid fiddling with my cock.

After dressing with a dolorous lethargy, I surveyed my appearance in the mirror. My blond hair, which I typically kept neat and clean, was in need of a wash, while my chin was in need of a shave. Those, naturally, were tasks of lower priority, given my present circumstances. My green eyes, normally keen and ebullient, now sunk a bit beneath heavy eyelids and above drooping, dark bags. I knew I was a handsome man, but in my current state, I had taken on a touch of Mr. Fairfield's melancholy complexion.

When I went downstairs, I skipped the kitchen and went straight to the drawing room, feeling no inclination toward another round of stop-and-go conversation with Mrs. Hawthorne. As Mr. Fairfield had taken upstairs with him the novel I had been reading the previous day, I plucked another one — I did not care which — from the shelf and sat down on the sofa. I opened the book, and my eyes scanned over the words without comprehending any of them. Although my thoughts were still vexing, I had ruminated so much upon them that they had become somewhat banal and insipid. And yet, I could not escape them.

For a half-hour, I maintained my post there before Mr. Fairfield finally came down. He materialized in the drawing room forthwith, dressed in the same ill-fitting raiment he had put on after his bath yesterday and looking particularly funeral.

"Mr. Hayward," he said to me in a serious voice, "would you be so kind as to join me in my apartment upstairs?"

"Of course, Mr. Fairfield," I replied. There was no need to sound collected, and I didn't. We both knew precisely what this was about.

I got to my feet and followed him upstairs, my body once more succumbing to the physiological symptoms of anxiety. However, there was a bit of succor to be found in the progression of the situation, knowing I would soon learn my fate.

When we reached the second-floor landing, I noticed the candle I had left there in the night was now gone, having no doubt been collected by Mr. Fairfield as further evidence of my treachery.

He led me directly into the room where I had found him during the night, and only with some exertion did I chase off the mental facsimile of his naked, masturbating body. The chair was still in the middle of the room, set in front of that full-length mirror by which I'd watched as he'd touched himself. The candles had been extinguished, but they remained flanked on either side of the seat, ready to be lit for his next round of self-indulgence. Mid-morning sunlight streamed in from the window, offering a more innocent glow, spurious as it was. In the distance, storm clouds gathered and loomed toward Bristlewood Manor. That was fittingly symbolic.

Mr. Fairfield proceeded to the chair, from which he picked up his mother's leather journal. He turned around and held it up in front of me.

"What is this?" he asked. His tone was not accusatory, but curious.

I swallowed and then replied. "It is a diary, sir."

He opened the book and thumbed through its pages. "I see that it is written in my mother's hand. I would know her calligraphy anywhere." Then he closed it and looked up at me. "Did you read it?"

"I did, sir," I said, figuring there was no sense in lying to him. Surely he was going to upbraid me no matter what I told him.

"And what did she write?" he inquired eagerly. "I saw my name on the first page, but I have enough trouble reading printed words. Needless to say, I could not decipher much from her calligraphy. Tell me everything."

"She wrote about," I began, resolved to be veracious yet circumspect in my wording, "your marriage to Virginia in that entry. And in the final one, she speaks of your daughter, Sophie."

Mr. Fairfield let out a long, stuttering sigh. His gaze dropped down to the journal in his hands, and he pulled away the cover to glance again at the first page. I could tell he was trying once more to read it, but quickly growing frustrated by the task, he dropped it back on the chair and asked, "And what were her sentiments on those subjects?"

"She was quite pleased by the news of both developments," I told him. "And she was … aggrieved by your distance from her."

His eyes flashed white hot at me. "She was aggrieved, you say?" he repeated, disdain now plain in his voice. "Some grief she must have felt! She never once wrote to me. She only ever addressed her letters to my uncle, and he never let me read them, nor did he ever tell me of their contents!"

Upon hearing him mention an uncle, I postulated that the Richard whom Mrs. Amelia mentioned must have been the same man. "Having read her words, sir," I said, "I cannot easily believe she did not want to write to you. In fact, at one point, I recall her lamenting that she did not receive any greeting from you in Richard's letters."

"Well, that is no great surprise," spat Mr. Fairfield with a malicious sneer. "My uncle is as cruel as my father was. That miserable bastard."

"It pained me to read, as well," I went on, "that your mother very much wished to visit you and your young family or even to bring you back here to Bristlewood Manor. She so desperately wanted to see you again and to meet your wife and daughter. But your father, it seems, would not allow it."

"Damn that bloody bastard straight to hell!" cried Mr. Fairfield viciously. He picked up one of the candles and threw it against a wall, smashing it into several pieces and sending the candlestick clattering across the floor. "I am glad he is finally dead!" he continued, clenching his free hand into a tight fist. "I only hope his death was slow and painful, and that the devil himself now torments him in the underworld!"

The fit startled me and caused me to take a few steps back from my pupil.

But upon seeing my alarm, he looked away, took a deep breath, and stopped himself from spewing more imprecations. He faced me again, and I saw that tears now glistened in his eyes. "I'm sorry," he breathed. Then he blinked, and the droplets began to fall. "The last time I saw my father was when I was eight years old, but even at that young age, he had already impressed upon me what a savage brute he was."

"I am so sorry," I said, knowing no other appropriate words to add.

"I'd tried to give him the benefit of the doubt. Maybe he and my mother didn't know how I'd toiled to get back into their good graces. Perhaps my uncle simply hadn't told them the lengths to which I went to be the son they actually wanted rather than the one they tried to forget. But now I learn that my father was aware, that my uncle did share the news, and yet, it made no difference. My uncle always told me how much my father hated me, but I'd hoped that would not be a permanent feeling. Or, at least, that my mother could soften him. But —"

Mr. Fairfield cut off and he succumbed to sobs. Covering his face with his hands, he fell onto his knees, wailing at the injustice he felt his life had been. I still didn't know what had turned Mr. William so intransigently against his son, his only child, but I saw in Mr. Fairfield's dejection that he, like his mother, had not deemed it so calamitous as to have never earned his father's pardon. Reduced now to weeping, with his face pressed into the floor, Mr. Fairfield had all but become again the eight-year-old boy who had been sent away so long ago.

The strictures of propriety could not restrain my compassion at that moment. I went right to Mr. Fairfield and knelt down before him, resting my hands on his shoulders as he mourned this new information about his mother's unrequited love for him. I thought I felt him relax the slightest bit at my touch, and I hoped the gesture could be some sort of palliative for a pain that nothing could truly fix. His suffering must have been quite profound if it could bring him down to this after such a short conversation, and in front of a veritable stranger, no less. So much for his being an intensely private man.

But I couldn't avoid considering my own shock at this scene. I had been prepared for an angry tirade directed at me for my infringement upon both Mrs. Amelia's diary and Mr. Fairfield's apartment. That he should become a blubbering mess in front of me was astounding, and yet, it left me encouraged as to the prospects of my continuing employment at Bristlewood Manor. That was a selfish thought, I know, but I'm sure you will understand and allow it.

After several minutes of crying, Mr. Fairfield brought himself up and sat back on his heels, his face coated with a mixture of fluids from his eyes, nose, and mouth. I let my hands fall from his shoulders and settled them in my lap, but he suddenly took hold of them and whispered, "Thank you."

"There is no need for gratitude, Mr. Fairfield," I responded, my fingers needling at his touch. I could not stop myself from recalling what those hands had been up to in the middle of the night. "I am only pleased that I could be of some assistance."

Mr. Fairfield gave me a small, glum smile as he released my hands and began wiping his face with his sleeves. "I am certain this is behavior quite unbecoming for a man of my station," he said, "and that, as my tutor, you must be appalled at me. But my sadness is so deep that it does not take much to make me cry these days."

"I am not appalled at you in the least bit," I assured him gently. "I can't imagine the pain the deaths of your parents have caused you, nor can I imagine the pain of your long separation from them."

"Believe me, I have experienced no pain at either the separation from my father or his death," he said with a croak. "But as for my mother, the pain of her loss is so great that I may as well grieve for two parents."

The corners of my lips turned up slightly at that. "She seems like she was a wonderful woman."

"She was the best of women," he corrected. "I knew she could not have ceased to love me, no matter how Richard tried to make it seem that way. She was the best of mothers, and she would have been the best of mothers-in-law and grandmothers if only she had been given the chance."

"Forgive my imprudence, sir," I said, "but may I ask you, where are Virginia and Sophie now? It seems you have not brought them to Bristlewood Manor."

Mr. Fairfield closed his eyes momentarily, then suddenly he got to his feet and walked away from me toward the window. He stopped in front of it, surveying the shoddy grounds his father had left him.

It seemed as if he were debating whether to broach this part of his life with me. I couldn't have blamed him if he sent me away without anything further, but, as I knelt on the floor watching him, I silently beseeched him to spill his secrets.

"No, I have not brought them to Bristlewood Manor," he said after a time. "I suppose you must be wondering why that is, and you will think something awful about me if I leave you in the dark about it."

"I would not think something awful about you," I assured him, "but I would like to know."

He looked at me momentarily, took in a deep breath, and went back to surveying out the window. "I told you that my sadness runs deep," he said. "I had barely enough time to know my daughter before some disease of infancy stole her away from me a month after she was born. Virginia was so devastated by Sophie's death that her health rapidly deteriorated, and she died within a fortnight. Then, a few weeks later, I received word of my mother's passing."

"My God," I breathed. So much loss in such a short period of time!

Mr. Fairfield continued as if he hadn't heard me. "I pleaded with the heavens to let my own heart fail me the way Virginia's had failed her. I was in the midst of being crushed by the weight of so much grief all at once, you understand. But I received no such mercy. That seems to be the theme of my life." He paused, letting out a bitter snort. "And to think, I only married her to gain my father's approval. I only sired a daughter to further prove to him that I was worthy of it. And not only did he refuse to offer me any sort of olive branch, but I could not even keep my two girls from death."

"You didn't marry Virginia out of love?" I asked, only realizing after speaking the question the potential impertinence of it.

"Oh, I loved her," he replied, turning and trodding back toward me. "I loved her dearly. But it was not the kind of love a husband has for his wife, though that was our arrangement. Rather, I loved her as one would love a precious sister or a very special friend. Make no mistake: she was my everything. But there were certain … facets of our marriage that were difficult for me. In particular, conceiving a child, you understand."

His meaning was not at all lost on me, for I expected that I would have faced the same challenges if ever I were to marry, and for that reason, I had decided not to do so. This revelation of Mr. Fairfield's may not have caught the attention of a man with natural predilections, but, to me, it was overwhelmingly significant. It led me to suspect Mr. Fairfield may not have been too upset about my watching him the night before.

"I understand you completely, sir," I declared. Although I had not planned to say it aloud, I did not regret it. For so long I had concealed this truth about me that it was such a relief to finally speak of it, albeit evasively.

"I had deduced as much," said Mr. Fairfield, fixing me with a stare like he could see through my clothes. I thought he would expound on his statement, but he didn't. Instead, he changed the subject, asking, "Did my mother mention in her diary why my father sent me away?"

"She did not," I replied, an impatient anticipation surging up in my chest and shoving aside the consternation of our mutual disclosures.

"That is not at all surprising," he said with a shrug and a roll of his eyes. "They were so ashamed of what I did. They were so afraid of anyone discovering it, for it would have surely been an end to their good reputation. I suppose she must not have dared commit it to paper, even more than a decade after the fact."

He began to nervously pace back and forth in front of the window, his shoes thumping against the floor with each step. He clasped his hands behind his back, and his fingers wriggled with jittery energy.

"I was eight years old, you remember," he began. "I was playing in the woods behind Bristlewood Manor, which I did often back then. But on that specific day, I heard a very queer noise, one that was unfamiliar to me. Young as I was, I thought that perhaps it was an injured animal, so I followed the sound to its source so I could rescue it. It so happened that it was not an animal, after all, but rather, ... an animal act, I should say. I found two men, both of them completely naked and unashamed of their bodies. They were lying on the ground within the branches of a low-hanging evergreen tree, assuming no one would find them there. And no wonder they had tried to conceal themselves, for they were doing all sorts of curious things to one another's bodies, particularly to each other's private parts. Most people would have found it repugnant. However, it fascinated me in a way that nothing ever had before. I kept hidden and watched them closely for a long time, until they finished up, got dressed, and left.

"When I went home, I couldn't shake the images from my mind. For weeks, they kept dancing in my head whether I wanted to relive them or not. Even when I was asleep, they appeared in my dreams. I saw them constantly, and I especially enjoyed the memory of their maleness. I was very fond of drawing back then, so I began revisiting the experience through art. I built up quite a collection of the naughtiest illustrations, and I confess I yearned to partake of those joys with another man someday. Each time I drew a new picture, the bodies and faces were of the men I'd seen that day, but in my head, they represented me.

"But one day, a housemaid stumbled upon them, and being so horrified by what they depicted, she brought them to my father. He flew into a rage and beat me severely, screaming on and on about how vile I was and about how he would not have a sodomite for a son. And then, next I knew, he shipped me off to work with my uncle in Antigua. I suppose it was to fix whatever was broken within me.

"I understood that what I had done was wrong, and I accepted the consequences of my behavior. I was determined to change, to become what God had apparently designed men to be. I did not want to be a sodomite, although, at that time, I had no idea what that was; I only knew it was something very, very wicked. I never drew again, but I couldn't stop myself from recreating that scene in my mind. I never dared to act out my urges with another, but I regularly defiled myself with my own hands.

"I thought my exile would be temporary, but as the years passed, I soon lost hope of returning home. And yet, I continued to fight against myself, suppressing my true desires in favor of what I had been taught was right and natural and good. All so that my father would forgive me. That was why I married Virginia and begat Sophie. And even so, my father did not forgive me, and my wife and daughter, who were the only sources of joy in my life, died. All of that pain and suffering simply because, as a boy, I was captivated by the sight of two men in sexual congress and decided to draw it. I can no longer trust in a God who would let that happen. I can no longer believe in the standard of what is right and natural and good given by a God who would allow so much wickedness on account of that standard."

Mr. Fairfield quit his monologue and his pacing simultaneously. He looked at me for a response.

I had listened to his story steadfastly, and I had been so moved by it that I could have cried if I'd granted myself license. But his blasphemy also flustered me. However, it was not because I found it scandalous or unwarranted, but because it had the ring of truth.

"I do not know what to say," was my only reply. I wondered why he was even telling me all of this, especially since he still barely knew me.

But perhaps I did know, even if I tried to dismiss the thought.

"And how could you know what to say?" rejoined Mr. Fairfield. "You must surely think I am a sinful lowlife bound for the pits of hell. And quite deservingly so. Is that not true?"

"On the contrary," I said, the tips of my ears burning, "I think you are a … kindred spirit." I knew I shouldn't have said that, but I couldn't help it. I'd never met another man like me, and that commonality was provocative and refreshing.

Mr. Fairfield smirked at me, which was quite jarring given the state of despair into which he had collapsed not more than ten minutes ago. "Yes, of course, I am," he said, almost musing to himself. "Surely you are well aware that I know you were watching me last night. Yes?"

"Yes," I breathed, unable to think of a convincing lie and unsure I even wanted to try.

"And I know you greatly enjoyed what you saw," he said, glancing over to the doorway where I had stood. "I *tasted* your enjoyment of it."

I didn't want to interpret the inference he made, but I did not have to. I comprehended it immediately. For those less astute readers: he was alluding to the semen I had left in his apartment and suggesting he had licked it up.

"I'm sorry, Mr. Fairfield; please, forgive me," I began, getting to my feet. "I know I was not supposed to be on the second floor at all, but I was frightened by the noises I heard in the night. I didn't know it was you making them. I'm embarrassed to admit that my imagination quite ran away with me, and in my state of fear, I felt compelled to investigate."

Mr. Fairfield bent toward me in a slight bow. "My apologies for interrupting your sleep, Mr. Hayward," he said courteously. "That must have been quite frustrating. And, as you say, frightening. I hadn't realized I could be heard on the third floor. Mrs. Hawthorne stays on the first floor, and she is practically deaf at this point, so it has never been an issue before. And as for your entering the second floor, I overheard Mrs. Hawthorne tell you on the day you arrived you were forbidden to do so. I might have forgiven you if only you had announced your presence last night and offered me the … pleasure of your company. But even as I say that, I think I must sound far too much like my father, so I will instead offer you a second chance."

"Erm, thank you, sir, that is most magnanimous of you," I replied, uncertain what he meant by "a second chance."

"Please, Mr. Hayward, if you are going to use fancy vocabulary, you should at least have the decency to define it for me," said Mr. Fairfield. "I am still your pupil, after all."

"Oh, yes, right," I fumbled. "To be magnanimous is to be merciful or forgiving."

"Thank you," said Mr. Fairfield. "It is such a pleasure to learn from you."

"Of course, sir, that is why you hired me," I sputtered.

"Indeed, it is. But I have no desire to be the type of man who treats those in my employ as mere objects of service while denying their humanity. And you should know, Mr. Hayward, I find your humanity quite … unmistakable."

"I am sure I haven't the slightest clue what you mean, sir," I fibbed, feeling nonplussed.

"Oh, I think you do," said Mr. Fairfield, gaping at me. "You said it yourself: you and I are kindred spirits. You and I are a unique breed of men, of whom there seem to be so few in the world. We are compelled to do things that would make a hardened war veteran blush like a schoolgirl. I maintain that those desires cannot be wrong. It would be such a shame to waste our acquaintance. Do you not think so?"

My legs began to weaken as I stood across the room from him, perfectly comprehending his innuendos. But I must own that I was scared. As much as I craved to relent to Mr. Fairfield's advances, the terror of committing so heinous a sin inhibited me from acting or even, now, speaking.

Clearly reading the reticence of my expression, Mr. Fairfield said, "But I see that you are hesitant. And that I can certainly understand. The powers that be have so forcefully instilled the fear of hell in us that they do not allow us to 'taste and see' for ourselves, as the psalmist put it, I believe. I may not be able to read well, but I have heard enough sermons for a lifetime."

"As have I," I said, my tongue loosened by a slightly different topic. "My father is a clergyman."

Mr. Fairfield dipped his head in acknowledgment. "Ah, yes. And for a son of a clergyman, to be what you are must be doubly disturbing."

I shrugged my shoulders, suddenly finding myself taciturn again. I did not like that phraseology: "to be what you are."

"I have no desire to force you into doing something you are uninterested in, Mr. Hayward," Mr. Fairfield went on. "I respect that your experiences have guided you, as have mine."

"It is not that I am uninterested, sir," I said. "It is that … I am afraid."

Mr. Fairfield smiled, but it was not a suggestive smile. Rather, it was understanding and a bit mournful. "The world is quite skilled at making us afraid. I can only speak for myself when I say that, having gone through what I have, I am no longer willing to submit to any authority outside of myself."

"That is a lovely thought in theory, Mr. Fairfield," I countered, "but does it not strike you as somewhat dangerous in practice?"

"For some people, perhaps. But, while there is much I do not know – and again, that is why I have hired you – I do know myself. If I may quote scripture again, I am a 'man of sorrows,' and that sorrow has made me a man of compassion as well. I need no external edict to keep me from lying, cheating, stealing, or killing. And my compassion must necessarily extend to myself. My father offered me none, so I must take up the responsibility now. In showing compassion to myself, I must no longer deny myself the true longings of my heart, even if those true longings are detestable to the rest of the world. The rest of the world does not know my heart as I do, and therefore, their opinion doesn't matter to me."

Now, it was my turn to smile. Whatever Mr. Fairfield may have lacked in education and whatever hardships he had endured, he was a decent, thoughtful man. "Perhaps, in the course of our professional acquaintance, I may learn from you as well," I said.

I did not mean it to sound like an insinuation, for I only meant to refer to the opportunity to engage with him philosophically. However, it is true that I was finding it harder to scorn his overtures. His contention in favor of self-indulgence was, I must say, quite cogent. Of course, the party most thoroughly convinced so far was my penis, and its … influence, shall we say, was only growing.

"I hope you will," returned Mr. Fairfield. "And if not, at least you shall still have those one hundred pounds a year."

I made myself laugh. "That is a sum I quite look forward to."

He smiled, and then he dropped his gaze to my crotch, clearly taking note of the burgeoning erection in my trousers. I had expected to be horrified at being caught like that, but I wasn't. Instead, I was energized, which did not stymie the effusion of blood flowing into my cock.

Mr. Fairfield's blue eyes bounced back up to mine, and he licked his lips ambivalently. "Forgive me, uh, I was … momentarily distracted. What were you saying?"

"I … I do not recall," I replied, feeling my self-control slipping away. Having him eye me like that had flipped some sort of switch in my mind.

Then I looked down too, and if I was not mistaken, I thought I saw movement in Mr. Fairfield's pants as well. That reintroduced the image of him in that chair, of his body, of his lust. Suddenly, I could not breathe. I could almost feel every drop of blood in my veins as they coursed through my body.

"Well, uh, then, in that case, perhaps we ought to take up our reading lesson again?" asked Mr. Fairfield with a skittish stutter.

You'll remember, dear reader, that scripture commands us to "Flee fornication." But elsewhere, it tells us "to eat, and to drink, and to be merry," and, as Mr. Fairfield had said, to "taste and see." At that moment, however, I could not consolidate any Bible passages into something approaching meaningful guidance. I was surmounted by yearning and spurred on by impulse. Voluble thought evanesced, and all that remained was urgency.

"Well," I said in barely more than a whisper, as if I could keep the almighty from eavesdropping, "I was thinking that perhaps … you could give me an introductory lesson in how to have compassion for one's self?"

Mr. Fairfield understood me right away, his eyes flaring up with salacity. "But are you certain?" he asked. "I do not want you to act in a way you will regret."

"I do not believe I shall regret a decision made in a heart full of love and compassion for myself," I replied, unsure from whence the words came. It didn't matter anyway. They were merely a pretense. "And if I do regret my choice, then, like the prodigal son, I shall throw myself at the father's feet and beg for his pardon."

"Then, perhaps we ought to remove to my bedroom," suggested Mr. Fairfield hoarsely. "That is the most appropriate place I can think of to begin our … lesson."

"I fully agree with you."

My fate now sealed, I went with him willingly and without questioning myself any further. I had been completely bewitched and was ready to concede defeat.

# CHAPTER TEN

Mr. Fairfield's bedroom had been stripped of any accoutrement that would have suggested to whom it had previously belonged, a fortunate realization I had considering what we were about to do inside of it. The room was furnished quite simply, not unlike my own up on the third floor, except that Mr. Fairfield's quarters were much more spacious and had a mattress fit for two sleepers in the middle of the right-hand wall. There was no art on the walls, and only a few lamps here and there – as well as the unmade bed – suggested that anyone spent time there.

After he had closed the door and turned the key, he spun to face me and stepped forward to take my hands in his. As he was not weeping this time, the touch of skin on skin felt like a bolt of lightning blasting through my whole body rather than a mere tingling sting.

"I must tell you," said Mr. Fairfield softly, "I have never done this before. I only know what I saw through a child's eyes that day in the woods, as well as the fantasies and dreams I had in the years after."

"Then you are still more educated on the subject than I am," I replied with an anxious chuckle. I did not know exactly what two men might do to each other in bed, but I was certain we would figure it out soon enough. After all, no one had taught me how to masturbate.

"And you're sure you want to do this?" he asked, squeezing my fingers tightly in his.

I grinned back at him, though I was wondering that myself. "Quit asking me that or I might change my mind," I said resolutely.

Laughing, Mr. Fairfield said, "Thank you for the warning. I would hate for you to reconsider. I very much want to do this." Then, his face turning sincere, he added, "I wonder if I might call you by your Christian name within this chamber, and if you might call me by mine."

"Certainly," I breathed, enamored of the thought of hearing my name pass his lips.

He smiled. "What is your Christian name, Mr. Hayward? I am afraid I cannot recall it."

"Edwin," I whispered.

"Edwin," he repeated, making something in my chest liquefy. "I am Halifax."

"Halifax," I said, appreciating the way the word needed both tongue and throat to form it.

We giggled together and then abruptly stopped at the same time, gazing into one another's eyes. I do not know who made the first, minuscule movement or if we acted simultaneously, but regardless, without another word, we brought forward our heads and pressed our lips together.

Oh, my dear, dear reader! It is now time for me to describe the sensation of that moment, and I find myself at a loss for words. Perhaps there are none. I could list several adjectives – such as magical, incredible, or transcendent – but I fear those would not quite capture it adequately. The physical delight itself was all of those things, but what I remember most vividly were the emotional and spiritual phenomena. It was as if I had been born anew, but this time into a body that was authentically my own. What had once been my shameful secrets were now my shared and finally realized yearnings. It was the experience of being truly myself, and with a co-participant to witness this blossoming.

Still locked in that passionate kiss, which now included the use of our tongues, we freed one another's hands to explore. Halifax's palms went straight to my buttocks, which he clutched as if they were his only means of survival in a roiling sea; what a joy it was to be touched there in a way that was not a beating! Meanwhile, my hands ended up on his chest, and before I had even made the conscious choice to do so, I had yanked off his ascot and was undoing the buttons of his shirt. Halifax briefly took his hands off of me to shed his coat and waistcoat himself. When he touched me again, he slid his hands down my back and into my trousers to grope my bare cheeks.

How I moaned at the sensation of his grip on my ass, reader! How I moaned!

But that did not distract me from my task. Within moments, I had doffed Halifax's shirt, revealing his torso. I pulled out of the kiss, not out of boredom or disgust, but because I wanted to turn my undivided attention to his chest. I planted my lips on his collarbone and meticulously moved over to the other one, leaving a trail of kisses in my wake. Then it was down to those lovely brown nipples. I pulled the left one into my mouth and washed it with my tongue, making Halifax gasp aloud. The teat bloated against my lips.

As I continued toying with his chest, he removed my coat and waistcoat, tossing them on the floor like so much rubbish. I had finished with both of his nipples and was making my way down to his belly, leaving me hunched over before him, when he ripped my shirt out of my trousers, bunching it up around my neck. He ran his fingers down the length of my spine, causing a tingle to encompass my whole back. With one hand, I gripped his hip, and with the other, I took off my ascot and unfastened a couple of buttons on my shirt. Then I let it come off over my head.

He drew me up to my full height and, placing a hand on my breast, examined my upper body with a tender, loving look. I had to remind myself that I had gotten a bit of a headstart on him, having had the chance to see him naked – although "through a glass, darkly" – the previous night. He allowed his fingers to caress the thin hair on my chest and belly, and then he took me by the hand and led me over to the bed.

I lay flat on my back, and Halifax knelt down on the floor. He removed my shoes and socks, then stood up and denuded his own feet. I grabbed his hand and tugged him onto the mattress with me, where we arranged ourselves side-by-side, resting our heads on the pillows. There we resumed kissing and feeling each other's bodies with our fingers. I soon learned I had quite the penchant for pinching his pretty, little nipples, and, as I did that, his hand traveled down over my belly to my crotch, which he massaged through my trousers. No doubt he was quite pleased to find I was already rather hard when he got there.

That inspired my next move. I imitated him, but as my hand passed down his smooth, slim body, I slipped my fingers under his trousers. Moving further in, I first encountered a forest of bristly hair and kept going a few inches until I collided with the firm base of him, which made my own cock jump. I walked my fingers to the right, following the glossy path formed by the hard shaft of his phallus, which had been diverted off to the side by his tight pants. When I reached the tip – which was still mostly sheathed in its foreskin – I wrapped my hand around my pupil's penis, gauging its thickness, memorizing its contours, and feeling out the softness of the skin and the unforgiving rigidity underneath. I found that it had more girth than I had given it credit for the night before.

All the while, I could not help thinking, "Dear God! I am actually touching a man's prick!" It had been my darkest dream for as long as I could remember, and to finally realize it with him was surreal. The sensation of another cock in my hand was better than I'd ever imagined it would be. It made my own stiff phallus strain against my pants.

There was not enough space inside his trousers for me to really stroke him the way I wanted to, so I returned to the base of his cock and moved downward to palpate the delicate skin of his scrotum and measure the ovals within. It was a more than satisfactory alternative.

During the time I spent with my hand deep in his pants, Halifax had been simultaneously teasing my nether region over my pants and unhooking the four buttons that ran down the front. Once he had concluded the latter task, he rolled over on top of me – which forced me to revoke my hand from the inside of his trousers – and began to kiss, lick, and bite me all across my chest, traversing downward as he did. When he arrived at my nipples and sucked them, an ineluctable cry burst from my throat, and a chill raced through my spine, expanding out to the tips of my fingers and toes. The stimulation was almost too much for me, but I did not want Halifax to stop, not when there was so much more yet to be done.

Nor did he. Not until he had migrated across the entire expanse of my torso and disembarked at the top of my trousers. Placing his hands on either hip, he slid his fingers inside the waistline of my pants. He slowly brought them down my legs and all the way off my feet in one motion, leaving me fully and manifestly naked in front of him. Once more, I had that sensation of being born and met again as he gaped at all of me, especially at my stiff, bare phallus, which throbbed with so much desire beneath his eyes. I could almost feel his pupils focusing on me, and I felt truly known for the first time in my life.

As if heeding an irresistible bidding, Halifax snatched up my cock with his hand, the first time anyone had ever grasped me there. It made me howl. He watched closely like a scientific researcher as he stroked me up and down, up and down, up and down. Unlike his, my foreskin always rolled back when I became aroused, freeing my red, triangular glans. But he quickly discovered – as I had, in my early days of adolescence – that, with the proper manual prompting, the prepuce would deftly glide over my head and back, an exercise that tickled me delectably. I observed how he touched me with those tall, slender, beautiful fingers, and I could not help but notice how he admired the eminent extent of my tool – it was fully seven inches in length, if not a smidgen more than that, and with a certain thinness that made it appear still longer. I loved seeing how he played with my stand the way a child might play with a new toy. I have confessed to you before that I felt a certain attraction to my own naked body, and it overjoyed me now that someone else could experience it too.

After a minute or two of this manual treatment, he made eye contact with me, smirked, and then bent down, taking my wooden prick in his mouth. This was better than anything my hand had ever done to me. My toes clenched of their own accord as his mouth and tongue writhed across my shaft and glans. He held the base of my cock steady with one hand, and with the other, he handled my balls and sack. I tousled his hair with my fingers as he bobbed up and down on me.

"Oh, my God, Halifax!" I moaned, pinching myself with my free hand to ensure this was not a dream. It was real. This was happening. "Your mouth feels so good on my prick! Oh, God!"

He removed his hand from my erection and used it to help himself wriggle out of his trousers. Once they were shucked off, he continued to suck me. With him now posed on all fours between my legs, my view of his full, naked body was occluded. I sat upright without withdrawing my member from his mouth and reached my arm around him to clutch his liberated cock. As I freely masturbated him, feeling how his hood slipped with some effort, I stared at the downhill slope of his fetching, firm ass. With my other hand, I clasped each fleshy cheek in turn, and then I traced a finger along his crack as far as I could reach, feeling all the fine, hidden hairs that marked out my trail.

I could have stayed like that forever: with him fellating me, and with me stroking his cock and fondling his ass. But after several minutes, I wanted more. I wanted to do to him what he was doing to me. I grabbed his chin and pulled him up. Understanding my wishes, Halifax dropped my penis from his mouth and slithered toward my face, pressing our bare bodies together. He kissed me, and as he did so, his hips squirmed, rubbing our vulnerable cocks together with the saliva he had left on mine acting as a slick lubricant.

We basked in that sublime position for a while, and then I shoved him over on his back and got on top of him. I did not coquettishly kiss my way down to his midsection. Instead, I knelt between his knees and scanned his fantastic naked body up and down, this time with the assistance of daylight and a straight-on angle to unmask it all before me.

His manhood rested enticingly on his belly, the skin of his prick slightly darker than the pallor of the rest of his body. It was, perhaps, an inch shorter than mine, but a bit thicker in girth. Whereas my cock was perfectly straight in its erect state, his had a slight upward curve to it. His scrotum hung loosely between his legs, which was quite unlike mine, for mine always held its contents closely and jealously.

I reached out a finger to touch the small bit of purple flesh poking out from the foreskin, then brushed him along the underside of his shaft, down his balls, and over his perineum, stopping when I reached the opening of his ass. I gently prodded his hole, which elicited a guttural croak from Halifax's throat and a noticeable concussion in his cock. I chuckled gleefully at my ability to create such an animal reaction in another man.

But that was enough of the teasing; I was ready to sample his prized components. To truly "taste and see." Lying down on my stomach with my face so close to his most private region that I could smell its appetizing aroma, I extended my tongue to sample his satiny sack. Reversing the trail that I had blazed with my finger, I licked him between his balls and up his wooden shaft. Once I reached the head, I nibbled at his foreskin with my lips. Then I opened my mouth and employed my tongue to pull his cock inside.

No element of any Christmas feast had ever tasted so delicious to me as his penis did right then. I was utterly infatuated with it. I swirled my tongue around his prick, analyzing and committing to memory every detail. I never wanted to forget that moment, that flavor, that feeling, that intimacy. As I sucked his cock, I let my finger travel back down to the darkness underneath him, and I resumed petting his asshole. Halifax groaned in pleasure, and as I gulped at him, I watched him lean back and close his eyes in what may otherwise have looked like a drug-induced stupor.

But I knew it was nothing of the sort. The only thing instigating that euphoria was my mouth around his penis and my finger on his hole. If my cock could have solidified any more, that thought would have made it happen.

A few droplets bubbled out of his piss slit and onto my tongue. I relished the savory taste of that small bit of prick fluid, knowing it was merely the forerunner to a much grander deluge. I desperately longed to open that floodgate and make him erupt in my mouth. Toward that end, I spat his cock from my mouth and caught it in my hand. I vigorously stroked it, which pulled down his foreskin enough to give me a full view of that excellent mushroom-shaped head. The sloshing sound of my saliva between my hand and his penis joined the chorus of his ecstatic cries, which were now a replica of those that had so terrified me my first two nights at Bristlewood Manor.

"Ahh—ahh—ahh—ahh—ahh—ahh—ahh—ahh—ahh—ahh—*Oh*!"

At that last affected shriek, his upper body jerked and all his muscles tightened. Realizing what that meant, I plunged his cock back into my mouth, and a half-second later, he filled my gullet with his hot, salty semen. I slurped out as much of the sacred juice as I could, savoring every single drop of him.

When Halifax's penis had at last quit oozing and I felt it begin to soften in my mouth, I released it and pushed myself up onto my hands and knees, proving to him that I was still quite erect and much in need of attention.

With a devious smirk, Halifax sat up and kissed me, thrusting his tongue into my mouth to test the flavor of his seed. Then he took me by the armpits and threw me over on my back. Sitting between my calves, he brought up his legs, picked up my cock with his bare feet, and commenced kneading me with them. It was not quite the same sensation as a hand or a mouth, but the exotic quality of it was exhilarating. Although I had never considered feet in a sexual context before, the feeling of Halifax's silky soles rubbing my penis made me dribble out some beads of my own liquid harbinger. And, I found, to my amazement, that his bony, paper-white feet were really quite beautiful. Stunningly so, in fact. The long, lanky toes — each with a couple of brown hairs sprouting from the knuckle — suddenly seemed very phallic to me, and the rounded, rectangular shape of their nails seemed very erotic.

But Halifax soon dropped his feet back to the bed and, puffing from the strain, said, "I can only do that for so long. I have not the muscles necessary to keep it up."

"That is quite all right," I replied with a grin. "Surely you have other parts with which you can please me."

"Oh, yes, I most certainly do," he whispered sensuously.

With that, he crawled up along the bed toward my head. I thought he was going to kiss me again, but instead, he spun around and planted his knees on either side of my hips. That left his ass directly in front of my face. Folding his body forward so his cheeks spread wide open before me, he started sucking on me again, his tongue splaying over every centimeter of surface area on my cock. Bathed in pleasure, I gawked at his exposed pink hole and felt a commanding urge to taste that precious part of him too. And why not? This whole day had been one of discovery, after all. So I clutched his fine ass, lifted up my head, and pressed my face between his cheeks. I kissed his hole as fervently as I had his lips, digging my tongue into him.

I had not expected his aperture to be so succulent, but it was. That I was wielding my mouth on this most forbidden of bodily orifices made it even more electrifying. It evidently had some effect on Halifax as well, for, though his penis was, by then, totally flaccid, he whimpered through his nose as he continued to orally provoke me.

Then, he changed his tactic. Keeping his mouth wrapped around my bald glans, he enveloped my shaft in his hand, sucking and stroking me at the same time. He did not get in more than four or five up-and-down motions before I felt it.

"Oh, Halifax!" I cried. "I am going to —"

And then, before I could finish announcing it, I did, unloading my pent-up semen into his mouth in several thick bursts. He swallowed all of it with a satisfied moan. Then he emancipated my cock and lay down on the bed beside me, both of us naked, drained, and gasping for breath.

# CHAPTER ELEVEN

Do you remember your first liaison with a partner, dear reader? How was it when you had both been satisfied? Did you fall asleep in one another's loving arms, or did you merely put on your clothes again and go about the rest of your day's business? I only hope your experience was not like mine. For, you see, as soon as I had spent, I disembarked from the height of sexual exaltation and alighted in a full panic.

"What was that?" I gasped, sitting up on the bed and scrambling to pull the covers over my nude self. I could have sworn on my father's thoroughly exercised Bible that I had caught the sound of a foot in the corridor on the other side of the door.

Meanwhile, outside, thick, gray storm clouds had stifled the sunlight and now ominously oppressed the bedroom where we lay.

"What are you talking about?" asked Halifax, who still lay relaxed on the mattress beside me.

"I thought I heard someone in the hall," I replied, turning to him with wide eyes. I was convinced we had been discovered and that we would, in due time, hang for our crime. "I know I heard someone. I am certain of it!"

Halifax grasped my shoulder and tried to draw me back down onto the bed, but I would not budge. Upon meeting my resistance, he said, "No, there is most certainly no one out there. The only other person in the house is Mrs. Hawthorne, and she only comes up to bring me my supper. She hasn't the legs to make multiple trips in a day."

That did not mollify my sudden terror. "But what if someone else gained entry to the house?" I cried.

He cocked an eyebrow at me, his handsome countenance twisting in an expression of concern. "Edwin, please calm down," he cooed. "There's no reason for anyone else to try to break in. I assure you, there's no one here besides us and Mrs. Hawthorne." Then he got up from the bed, traipsed over to the door, unlocked it, and flung it wide, apparently so confident there was no intruder that he had no scruple about standing in front of the open doorway without concealing his nudity. And indeed, there was no one there. "You see? We are alone."

Perhaps that should have been enough to appease me. However, I was still deeply unsettled, but it seems I was almost fabricating reasons to still be afraid. "And what if the noise I heard was the sound of someone sneaking *away* from here? By the time you opened the door, they could have been long gone."

"I very much doubt it," said Halifax, shutting the door with a sigh. "Bristlewood Manor is not what it used to be, and I think anyone who wanted to rob a large mansion could find much better options." He returned to the bed, and I turned my eyes so as not to ogle his body as he did. He crawled on top of the mattress, leaning in to kiss me.

I pulled away from him in revulsion. "Please, don't," I said. Even if no human had been monitoring us, I knew there had still been a witness. God saw everything, and no locked door could prevent his constant surveillance.

With a jilted look, Halifax beheld me for a moment, as if by studying my face he could better understand me. "What is happening right now, Edwin?" he whispered tenderly, resting his hand on my shoulder. "You are starting to scare me."

I squirmed away from his touch as if it burned. I could feel myself starting to come unraveled, my sanity starting to fray.

"I do not know," I said in a shaky voice.

I shoved off the covers and got to my feet. Like Adam and Eve, I was abruptly ashamed of my nakedness, and I covered my bare genitals with my hand. My pubic hair tickled my palm, reminding me of the old wives' tale about what would happen to chronic masturbators. My legs felt weak underneath me as I went about the room, collecting my clothes from the floor.

"What are you doing?" he asked, drawing himself up onto his knees, watching me.

Having gathered up everything I had worn into the room, I set it all on the bed, then took up my trousers first. "I am getting dressed," was my only explanation, for I could not give a full account of all the horridly guilty thoughts in my head.

He was clearly disappointed at that. "But why? Can we not engage in today's education in this room, wearing nothing? It sounds extremely pleasant, do you not think so?"

Still hiding myself behind one hand, I used the other to awkwardly hold out the pants and stepped my feet into them. I pulled them all the way up, then turned away from Halifax so I could employ both hands in the task of buttoning them without exhibiting my private parts. There was no avoiding him seeing the top of my nude ass.

"That would be most improper," I said, rotating back toward the bed to retrieve my shirt.

"How so? We have already done far more than that."

"It would be most improper," I repeated.

"According to whom?"

"According to everyone except you, apparently," I exclaimed sternly, putting on the shirt and buttoning it all the way up. Seeing how shocked he was by my tone, I forced myself to soften it and added, "I'm sorry, sir. I should not have spoken to you that way."

Halifax ignored my apology. "Do you now regret what we have done? You told me you did not think you would regret a decision made out of compassion and love."

A loud clap of thunder made me jump as I adjusted my ascot. A moment later, there was a flash of lightning, and rain began to tap against the windowpane. All of it seemed to be a divine declaration of awareness and accusation.

Taking a deep breath to recollect myself, I said, "It was not right."

Halifax leaped up from the bed in a huff of fiery anger. "Do not say these things to me!" he bellowed, causing me to stumble backward in alarm at the precipitous change in his tone and his dark glower. "I will not abide the attitudes of my father being expressed in this house. He is dead. I am the master of Bristlewood Manor now!"

Another peal of thunder boomed, emphasizing his declaration.

"My apologies, sir," I returned, my voice belying the quaking fear that affected my entire body. I grabbed my shoes, socks, coat, and waistcoat without putting them on. "I must be going now. Good afternoon."

And I fled the room, my bare feet pounding the floor just as they had the previous night.

It was the sound of disgrace.

Mr. Fairfield did not pursue me up to my room on the third floor, nor did he call anything after me. And thank God he did not!

I closed the door behind me, dropped my shoes, coat, and waistcoat, and fell to my knees on the floor. The wind howled outside my window as I clasped my hands in contrition, pleading with the heavens.

"Lord Jesus Christ, son of God, have mercy on me, a sinner," I recited, the prayer having never been so poignant before. "Lord Jesus Christ, son of God, have mercy on me, a sinner. Lord Jesus Christ, son of God, have mercy on me, a sinner. Lord Jesus Christ, son of God, have mercy on me, a sinner. Lord Jesus Christ, son of God, have mercy on me, a sinner. Lord Jesus Christ, son of God, have mercy on me, a sinner."

Tears streamed down my face, but as the storm continued to rage outside, I did not feel anything like divine mercy. Perhaps, I thought, my sin was undeserving of mercy. The earthly powers had deemed it as such by attributing capital punishment for the offense, and I believed then that the laws of the British Empire had been guided by providence. And if there was to be no mercy for me, I could not protest.

As I thought back to the nauseating things I had done in Mr. Fairfield's bedroom, it almost felt like a dream or like the hazy memory of a book I had read many years before. I had always been so diligent about not falling into temptation with another person, about not letting anyone know I was attracted to my own sex. But I had just done both, one right after the other! I was certain I was the worst of all transgressors. How could anyone short of a murderer have deviated from the path of righteousness more critically than I had?

Shortly, I perceived that I was being watched. I spun around on my knees, assuming Mr. Fairfield must have soundlessly entered my room. But no, I perceived, he had not. No one had. I was all alone in those small quarters, and the door was still closed, just as I had left it. And yet, that awful feeling that someone was observing me persisted so strongly it may as well have been a proven fact, even without any sort of physical evidence. It went beyond the simple knowledge of God's omnipresence and omniscience; it was more palpable, more present, more haunting.

This time, I bowed my head to the floor, sobs shaking my shoulders as I entreated the almighty for his grace.

"Lord Jesus Christ, son of God, have mercy on me, a sinner."

"Sinnersinnersinnersinner!"

I bolted upright. The harrowing echo of the last word of my prayer reverberated back to me in a voice that was not my own, a voice of malice and inculpatory contempt. It must have been some sort of temporary madness caused by my tremendous guilt, surely, but somehow I knew I had just heard the ghost of Mr. William Fairfield accusing me.

I pressed my forehead to the ground again, pining for absolution.

"Lord Jesus Christ, son of God, have mercy on me, a sinner."

"Sinnersinnersinnersinner!"

The indictment startled me again, but I did not sit up and I did not stop praying.

"Lord Jesus Christ, son of God, have mercy on me, a sinner."

"Sinnersinnersinnersinner!"

"Lord Jesus Christ, son of God, have mercy on me, a sinner."

"Sinnersinnersinnersinner!"

"Lord Jesus Christ, son of God, have mercy on me, a sinner."

"Sinnersinnersinnersinner!"

And at last, I could bear it no more. With a wordless cry, I got to my feet and stomped over to the bedside table, taking from it my Bible. Opening it to Psalm 51, King David's canticle of lamentation over his adulterous sin with Bathsheba, I began to read it aloud as I paced the room, feeling every word of it acutely. This functioned somewhat as a magical incantation, for I did not hear Mr. William's voice again that afternoon.

"Have mercy upon me, O God, according to thy lovingkindness: according unto the multitude of thy tender mercies blot out my transgressions. Wash me throughly from mine iniquity, and cleanse me from my sin. For I acknowledge my transgressions: and my sin is ever before me. … Purge me with hyssop, and I shall be clean: wash me, and I shall be whiter than snow. Make me to hear joy and gladness; that the bones which thou hast broken may rejoice. Hide thy face from my sins, and blot out all mine iniquities. Create in me a clean heart, O God; and renew a right spirit within me. Cast me not away from thy presence; and take not thy holy spirit from me. …"

I continued to chant the psalm over and over again, both to drown out all voices but my own and with the hope that enough repetitions could wash me clean and free me of my guilt. But after I had intonated the ancient words five times through, I was exhausted and still burdened by my iniquity. It was as if I had committed the unpardonable sin, the one not even the prodigal son had dared to perpetrate.

I flipped through the book, seeking other comfort, but all I found was more condemnation:

"The wages of sin is death."

"The fearful, and unbelieving, and the abominable, and murderers, and whoremongers, and sorcerers, and idolaters, and all liars, shall have their part in the lake which burneth with fire and brimstone."

"If a man also lie with mankind, as he lieth with a woman, both of them have committed an abomination: they shall surely be put to death; their blood shall be upon them."

"The men, leaving the natural use of the woman, burned in their lust one toward another; men with men working that which is unseemly, and receiving in themselves that recompence of their error which was meet."

"Even as Sodom and Gomorrha, and the cities about them in like manner, giving themselves over to fornication, and going after strange flesh, are set forth for an example, suffering the vengeance of eternal fire."

Enough! Enough! Enough!

Setting aside the Bible, I returned to my knees. I began to pray in my own words, making a promise to God, not unlike Martin Luther, that if he would ransom me, I would never again degrade myself that way again.

However, even as I said the words, they felt disingenuous. I was afraid, not just of the consequences of my actions, but of their perpetuation. This was my pattern with vices, particularly those of the corporeal kind. After all, how many times had I sworn to the Lord I would never masturbate again? Now that I had been initiated into a new form of iniquity, I feared I would not be able to keep from violating the laws of God and nature again and again.

As it is written: "As a dog returneth to his vomit, so a fool returneth to his folly."

I was already so enervated by my ruefulness, and the notion of a daily crusade against a new, pervasive seduction was further disheartening. Getting up from the floor, I lay down on the bed and simply cried, hoping my tormented tears would be penitence enough.

# CHAPTER TWELVE

Throughout the scriptures, there are no less than a dozen (that I know of) great heroes of the faith who received brilliant visions from God. I would never count myself as a great hero of anything, much less of the faith, but I, too, had a vision. It was not one of those overpowering, phantasmagorical raptures in which the diviner witnesses the sundry glories of heaven. Mine was rather more like the dreams of Nebuchadnezzar, which had perplexed and terrified him to his very soul.

Mine was a nightmare of hell.

There were flames, yes, as well as a caustic, burning agony to go along with the mutilated shrieks of my fellow reprobates. But it was, somehow, bitterly cold and brutally silent at the same time. There was no end to the worsening gradations and increasingly inventive varieties of pain, and certainly no end to the pain itself. There was neither consolation nor solidarity to be found in the excruciating screams of others, for they only exacerbated my own suffering. I could hear them all, but not as sounds, for even in chaotic discord there may be some small measure of comfort in not being alone. But the greatest misery was that I was cosmically abandoned: unseen, unheard, unremarked, unloved by any and all, so much so that even the torture itself was passive. There was no devil present to mock me nor any demon specified to punish me, for that would have required me to have been noticed at all. Mine was a shred of an existence, only the bare minimum needed – and no more – to sustain the utmost affliction for all of eternity. To be simply annihilated would have been far too extravagant a mercy for a miscreant as twisted and perverted as me. I could not even complain, though, because there were no ears to hear and there was no one to blame but myself.

Sinnersinnersinnersinner!

Sinnersinnersinnersinner!

Sinnersinnersinnersinner!

Sinnersinnersinnersinner!

A knock at the door brought me awake. I was choking for breath, and my clothes were drenched in sweat. I was not in hell, but rather in the comparatively comfortable confines of my room at Bristlewood Manor. A torrent of relief passed over me. The dream had seemed so real I was almost surprised to find my skin was not severely charred, nor was it even a tiny bit singed.

It was still afternoon outside. The thunder and lightning had stopped, but a light rain continued to fall.

I was all right.

Relatively speaking.

There was another rap at the door. I'd been so fixed on realizing the nightmare had been completely illusory that I'd forgotten what had rescued me from it.

"Come in," I called out.

Mr. Fairfield opened the door and entered, fully dressed once more in his baggy clothes. Strange as it may seem to you, dear reader, until I saw him, I had yet to recollect the dream's precipitating event.

"Are you all right, Mr. Hayward?" he asked, dispensing with the use of my Christian name. He looked shaken, like he, too, had passed through some sort of distressing absorption.

"I was just sleeping," I explained, sitting up in bed. I was still barefoot and without a waistcoat from having fled his apartment without fully dressing, and that seemed a degree of intimacy that must now be categorized as wholly inappropriate.

"You were yelling in your sleep," said Mr. Fairfield. "I heard it from my apartment. It was a nightmare, then?"

I shook my head at him, uninterested in explaining the vision to him. "The quality of my sleep and the content of my dreams are irrelevant to any conversation you and I are to have, given our current professional relationship."

"Oh, come on, Edwin," he said, stepping up to me, exasperated. "You know things have changed between us."

I backed him off with a stern glower. Trying to maintain a semblance of composure and rectitude, I said, "If the nature of our affiliation has been altered, then perhaps it would be better if I left your employ."

"I would forbid it!" cried Mr. Fairfield, his anger rising suddenly. But then, he suddenly relaxed. "Forgive me. I should not have spoken to you like that. I'm sorry. As well as his blue eyes, my father also passed on to me his temper."

I said nothing in response. I'd dropped my eyes when he'd raised his voice, and now I couldn't even meet his gaze.

"Edwin, please," he went on imploringly, "I do not forbid your leaving, but I beg you not to depart. In the short time you have been at Bristlewood Manor, I have grown rather fond of you. And I don't just refer to what we did in the bedroom. I was fond of you even before that, and I would still be fond of you even if it had never happened. You were so patient and kind to me yesterday while helping me with my letters. And this morning, you were compassionate and understanding toward me in my grief. I have never experienced so much of that before, and the thought of losing it after such a small but powerful sampling is … unbearable."

As much as I hated it, my heart softened toward him with those words. He was, as he'd said earlier, a "man of sorrows," a man much in need of education, companionship, care, and, yes, love. All of those I had aspired to give him, albeit in a moral and upright way. But, it seemed to me, I had squandered all of that by accompanying him to his bedroom that morning. Or, before that, by trespassing in his apartment during the night.

"I'm pleased I could offer you what the world has so far neglected to grant you," I said evenly. "But those things must be given in the right way."

Mr. Fairfield's jaw tightened. "I told you not to speak like my father in my house," he said, his tone serious, though he strained to keep himself under control.

"I'm sorry," I replied, feeling caught. "But you must understand, I feel this awful guilt and shame over what we did."

I hadn't meant to share that with him, but I feared his wrath, and he had quite tied my hands by forbidding me to sound at all like Mr. William.

Never mind the fact I was the one who had been hearing Mr. William's voice.

"But why?" asked Mr. Fairfield. "Was it not pleasant and thrilling? Was it not beautiful and intimate?"

"It was all of those things and more," I said, biting my lip and hating the admission. "I don't know how to explain my feelings to you, sir, particularly since it is clear we hold very different beliefs about these things, and you don't wish for me to sound like your father."

I could not quite read Mr. Fairfield's face, whether he was angry or sad. Or perhaps he was both at the same time. "Very well then," he said, his voice resolute and dejected. "I have grown quite accustomed to ripe fruit spoiling. What is one more painful loss?"

"Mr. Fairfield, please, you must not speak that way," I chided him softly. "This present situation is very different from the others through which you have passed. Your parents are supposed to love you and forgive you and keep you. Your uncle is supposed to treat you with dignity and respect. Your wife and child are supposed to survive a long time by your side. But you are not supposed to have an affair with your tutor."

His mouth twitched. Even in his grimness, he was still so attractive. It crushed me to reject him like that, but I had no other choice. We couldn't continue as we had.

"Very well then," he repeated, straightening his spine. "You may have the rest of the day to yourself, as I can see you are rather…upset. But on the morrow, if you decide you will not quit my employ, I should like to take up my lessons with you again." Then, he clarified what he meant: "My *reading* lessons, that is. Will you stay? I pray you will."

"I will," I confirmed, although I had not yet had time to think through the matter as much as I should have. If I didn't trust myself to avoid future temptation, then staying at Bristlewood Manor was almost an open solicitation to the devil's wiles.

"Thank you, Mr. Hayward," he said with a deep bow, bending forward further than he ever had before. "I look forward to reading the next chapter of that novel. I must say, I am quite interested in it."

Then, he left the room.

You will forgive me, dear reader, for my excess of tears. It was quite an emotional day, as you have seen, and as soon as Mr. Fairfield shut the door behind him, I launched into another spell of weeping. However, on this occasion, my grief wasn't respecting the horror of my error. Perhaps it should've been, but it wasn't. I mourned, rather, that my error was categorized as an error at all. It gave the impression of sacrilege to think like that, for I, as I'm sure you were, too, had always been taught that God's laws were perfect and just, and therefore, any sorrow over the Lord's decrees could've only been the result of a wayward soul's wayward feelings. But I was sorry that what Mr. Fairfield and I had shared together was sinful because, as he'd said himself, it was pleasant and thrilling, beautiful and intimate. That something could feel so superlatively right and yet still be so emphatically wrong seemed, to me, a great travesty. I wished I could've had Mr. Fairfield's dispassionate attitude toward the whole matter, but I was too much my father's son to set aside the words of holy writ in favor of what I felt.

And for that, dear reader, I wept. I wept for a long time, and after my tears finally desisted, I got up and went downstairs. Having missed lunch, I needed to eat, and I did so without speaking much to Mrs. Hawthorne. I wondered if she could perceive the reason for my taciturnity.

Either way, I was certain she did not mind it.

I abnegated the reading of any fiction that evening, believing it to be an unearned, frivolous diversion. Instead, I perambulated the ground floor of Bristlewood Manor (it was too wet for a walk outdoors), praying further for mercy from my God as well as for divine fortitude and self-discipline in the coming days. When I finished that, I took from the bookshelf a collection of sermons from the last century and went straight to my bedroom. There, I pored over the words of God-fearing men until somnolence visited me.

The particularly unsparing words of an American preacher named Edwards haunted my dreams that night, and I copy an excerpt of them here to provide you with an inkling of my state of mind:

"The God that holds you over the pit of hell, much as one holds a spider, or some loathsome insect over the fire, abhors you, and is dreadfully provoked: his wrath towards you burns like fire; he looks upon you as worthy of nothing else, but to be cast into the fire; he is of purer eyes than to bear to have you in his sight; you are ten thousand times more abominable in his eyes, than the most hateful venomous serpent is in ours. You have offended him infinitely more than ever a stubborn rebel did his prince; and yet it is nothing but his hand that holds you from falling into the fire every moment. It is to be ascribed to nothing else, that you did not go to hell the last night; that you were suffered to awake again in this world, after you closed your eyes to sleep."

# CHAPTER THIRTEEN

I'd thought that my illicit tryst with Mr. Fairfield and my heartfelt ensuing emotions might've at least granted me a full night's sleep. But after I'd been asnooze for a few hours, his screaming woke me up again. Now, though, it wasn't terror that gripped me but anger. I was dreadfully tired, the result of sleeping poorly the two previous nights and of the volatility of the day that was, and being awoken once more was most provoking. And what made it worse was that I'd told Mr. Fairfield that morning he'd roused me in the night, and he'd apologized, saying that wasn't his intention and that he was not aware he could be heard from my quarters. And yet, here he was, at it again without any compunction. He'd already ejaculated in my mouth that day, so I'd thought he would've been quite spent and not in need of more midnight masturbation.

The knowledge that it was nothing supernatural didn't calm me enough to sleep once more, although I tried. And the fact that it seemed to persist far longer than it had ever before brought me near to seething. At a minimum, Mr. Fairfield was behaving quite inconsiderately, if not downright grotesquely. Had he not the most trifling measure of self-control?

Supposing it might be quieter somewhere else in the mansion, I got out of bed and, taking up the new candle I'd procured when I was downstairs earlier, left the room. I went down to the drawing room, having rolled my eyes at the strident clamor as I passed through the second-floor landing. Thankfully, the howling was quite a bit quieter, though still faintly audible, on the ground floor. Sitting on my regular sofa, I picked up the book I had been attempting to read before Mr. Fairfield had asked me up to his apartment that morning.

Ten minutes had passed, the yelling continuing all the while, when I heard something like a footstep outside, and I jolted in my seat. Telling myself it was just a paranoid hallucination like the one I'd apparently experienced earlier in Mr. Fairfield's bedroom, I tried to settle back down to read.

Only I heard another footstep. And then another. And another. Whoever the feet belonged to, they were approaching the house from behind. To come from that direction and at this time of night could have been nothing *comme il faut*, as they say.

I jumped to my feet, snatched the additional oil lamp I'd lit, and rushed to grab a poker from the fireplace to use as a weapon. My pulse was set to hammering for a third night in a row. Wearing only my nightclothes, I stepped out of the drawing room, brandishing the poker, just as the back door to Bristlewood Manor opened.

And in walked Mr. Fairfield.

"What the devil is this?" he cried, startled to see me standing there, wielding a crude club.

Feeling subdued now that I knew this was no malicious intruder – but quite vexed about Mr. Fairfield's presence there – I answered his question with two of my own. "What are you doing? How did you get out there?"

"I was out for a midnight walk, and I got out there by … walking through the door," explained Mr. Fairfield, evidently confounded by my queries. He stepped further into the house, and as he moved closer to the light, I saw that his boots, pants, hands, and even parts of his face were caked in mud. "What are *you* doing?"

"But how did —" I sputtered, unsure even how to rephrase my questions to make them more coherent. "But you were upstairs."

"I *was* upstairs," he began, "but then I came downstairs to go out. It was about an hour and a half ago, I should think. Now, please, answer my question, Mr. Hayward: What are you doing?"

At a complete loss for a cogent and reasonable response, I decided to just tell him the truth. "I came downstairs because I couldn't sleep thanks to all your yelling."

"All my yelling?" repeated Mr. Fairfield, his outward expression as confused as I felt inside.

"The yelling you do when you..." I made a gesture to represent frigging, unable to think of a more decorous word for it.

It was then I realized the screaming upstairs had stopped, which, of course, made perfect sense because Mr. Fairfield was standing right in front of me. But I hadn't noticed when they'd ended, and I last remembered hearing them as I left the drawing room with the fire poker in hand.

"But I have not done that today; I haven't had the need, you understand," said Mr. Fairfield. "And besides, as I said, I have been out for at least an hour and a half, if not more than that. You must have been mistaken."

Mistaken? But how was that possible? The wailing had been as clear as day, and it'd shifted in character when I'd changed my location in the house. That couldn't have been a blunder of hearing!

I was abruptly lightheaded, and I gripped the wall to steady myself on my feet. Mr. Fairfield rushed forward and wrapped his dirty hands around my wrists, keeping me upright. I hadn't even the presence of mind just then to despise the touch.

"Are you all right, Mr. Hayward?" he asked, staring straight into my eyes, searching for an explanation for my irregular behavior and odd claims.

"Yes, I'm fine," I lied, shaking my head as if to clear it. "Just … uh … just tired, I suppose."

"Then let's get you up to bed." After taking the fire poker from me and setting it aside, Mr. Fairfield wrapped his arm around my shoulder while continuing to grip my other arm. He then spun me around toward the front staircase, holding me solidly perpendicular. "You look in rather rough shape."

We walked together, his muddy boots thumping heavily on the floor while my bare feet slapped it. I didn't mind having him there to support me, for it allowed me to focus my attention on dissecting what had just happened. The problem was there didn't seem to be a logical solution. It should have been impossible for me to have heard Mr. Fairfield screaming upstairs at the very same time as he was entering the house from outside.

And yet, it was, to me, a dubious and gratuitous assumption that I had mistaken another noise for Mr. Fairfield's hollering, or that I had made it up altogether. Hearing a single, nonexistent footstep outside a bedroom door was one thing, but fabricating a persistent howling was quite another.

Well, then. Was it possible Mr. Fairfield was an identical twin, and that the twin, being otherwise locked up during the day, came out to masturbate whenever the brother went out at night? Or was the man assisting me up the stairs right now the twin?

No, no, that could not be. He'd seemed so familiar with me, had used my name, and had even made a passing reference to our earlier sexual encounter. But if this was the real Mr. Fairfield – the real Mr. *Halifax* Fairfield, that is – then would I find another man, who at least sounded exactly like him, zealously pleasuring himself in the room upstairs?

Well, probably not. The screaming had stopped, after all. Perhaps the other Mr. Fairfield had heard his brother coming back to the house, quickly gotten dressed, and fled back to his hiding place – or his cell. And anyway, I knew I couldn't investigate, for there was no way to concoct a pretext to enter his apartment for a look around without it seeming like a sexual advance.

So I said nothing at all to him, relying on my stupefaction as an excuse for my dumbness.

When he got me to my room, I was half-afraid he would be the one concocting a pretext to stay. But after I set the oil lamp on the bedside table and crawled under the sheets, he just nodded at me and said, "Good night, Mr. Hayward. I hope you'll feel better in the morning. I still look forward to my reading lesson."

Then he left.

Fatigued as I was, it took me a long while to get back to sleep. My mind was caught in a whirlwind of thought, but the tone was mostly of befuddlement. It appeared I had not yet disentangled all the mysteries of Bristlewood Manor.

# CHAPTER FOURTEEN

In the morning, after another wordless breakfast with Mrs. Hawthorne (much to her delight), I waited for Mr. Fairfield's apparition in the drawing room. But this time, I didn't even attempt to interest myself in that damned novel, and I put it back in its place on the bookshelf in disgust.

Thankfully, it did not take long for him to show up, looking fresh and clean after being so filthy the night before. He had brought down with him the book whose opening chapter we'd worked through in our first lesson two days prior.

We'd never gotten around to any instruction yesterday.

"Good morning, Mr. Fairfield," I said somberly.

"Good morning, Mr. Hayward," he replied, sounding overly pleasant, like he was forcing himself to sound that way.

He sat down directly beside me on the sofa without any dither. I nearly leaped up to move to the other couch when I remembered that this had been the arrangement the first time, albeit on the other side of the room. I relaxed my body but maintained a resolute focus on my knee and feet, lest they should drift over and touch his at any point.

We began by thoroughly reviewing the words we had marked out two days prior, and it was a good thing we did; Mr. Fairfield barely remembered the definition of any of them, and he even needed a reminder about the pronunciation of some. When that retrospective task had been concluded, I set him on a writing exercise, wherein I charged him to come up with two unique sentences for each of those words to demonstrate his mastery over their use. Only then, after I had taken a short break for lunch, did we move on to the book's second chapter.

The awkwardness receded as the hours passed, particularly when I perceived that Mr. Fairfield was sincerely trying (and struggling) with the words, and also when I automatically addressed him as a teacher and not as a lover. Our tutor-pupil relationship was genuine, if unique, and a bit tainted now, and I was quite assured we could continue it despite what had taken place between us yesterday.

And despite the oppressive guilt I still felt in response to it.

And despite my current, if loosely held, theorem that Mr. Fairfield had a secret twin brother — of whom neither he nor Mrs. Hawthorne had ever spoken, and of whom Mrs. Amelia had never written — who was locked away in the house somewhere and only came out to carry on loudly while masturbating in the middle of the night.

I quite understand your skepticism, dear reader, and I readily own that all of it was quite irrational. My father would have counseled me to "flee from temptation" and therefore, as Mr. Fairfield was still a definite temptation for me, to quit Bristlewood Manor. But my father was not there to tell me that, nor would I have ever disclosed to him what I had done with my employer. And so I stayed, believing that I, notwithstanding all my own concerns and faults, could effectively and single-handedly make Mr. Fairfield into a respectable gentleman.

That is not to say my eyes did not occasionally drift over to the crotch of Mr. Fairfield's trousers, attempting to ascertain the silhouette of his pretty little cock and balls. I certainly did that on a few occasions, at times voluntarily and at times impulsively. But I always caught myself when I felt that process of ossification begin in my own pants, and one time I was positive Mr. Fairfield caught me looking. He did not seem upset by it and said nothing, though I was embarrassed.

Late in the afternoon, we were interrupted by the sound of Mrs. Hawthorne bursting through the back door and doddering as fast as she could – which was not fast – to the drawing room. When she appeared, she was heaving for breath, her hair was a runaway mess, she was crying, and she looked on the verge of fainting.

At once, Mr. Fairfield and I leaped up and ran over to her. Then, each of us taking one of her arms, we led her to the sofa, where she deflated in a fit of emotion.

"Oh, Mr. Fairfield!" she cried breathlessly through gasps and sobs. "Your m–. Your mother–. Your mother's grave –. It has been – robbed!"

"What?" I exclaimed, wide-eyed and unbelieving.

Mr. Fairfield, who had sat down beside Mrs. Hawthorne and clung to her hand with his, said nothing.

"I was taking a walk in the woods to pay my respe–ects," she explained, still distressed and still huffing and puffing. "And as I got closer, I saw immediately that there was a pile of dirt beside your mother's resting place, and I thought it could not be, surely it could not be! But when I stepped right up to it, when I looked as close at it as I look at you now, I saw it was true! The earth had been dug up and her coffin was open but she –."

Here, she broke down into aggrieved laments, burying her face in her hands. But I did not need her to finish the sentence. I already knew what she had been about to say, and I assumed Mr. Fairfield had too.

I glanced over at him. He was impassive, save for that clenched jaw I had come to recognize as a harbinger of his temper. But certainly, in this case, I could not blame him for any umbrage. I was quite outraged myself, and it wasn't even my own mother.

"What are we to do?" I asked Mr. Fairfield.

"Nothing for now," he murmured quietly to me. Then to Mrs. Hawthorne, he added, "There, there, now, Mrs. Hawthorne. I'm sure you simply misapprehended the situation, that is all. Sometimes our grief can play strange tricks on our minds, and I can only imagine your grief must have been unbearable, having known my parents as well and for as long as you did. Hush, now, my dear. Everything is all right."

She pulled her hands away from her face, rapidly shaking her head at him. "No, no! It was not a fit of lunacy that came over me!" she cried indignantly. "I saw it! *I saw it!*"

My skin crawled and my body convulsed at the sound of her last, desperate shriek.

"All right, all right, shh, shh," cooed Mr. Fairfield sedately, patting and rubbing her on the back and kissing her on the forehead. "I can see how terribly you are upset, Mrs. Hawthorne. I think it would be good for you to lie down for a bit and regain your composure. I will handle this. You needn't worry any further."

Mrs. Hawthorne reluctantly assented to her master's suggestion, and we helped her to stand up on her jostling legs. I started to walk with them, but Mr. Fairfield waved me off, giving me a look that said it would be best if he managed this alone. Since I knew how little Mrs. Hawthorne cared for me, I nodded and returned to my seat on the sofa. Like a sedulous nurse, he gingerly guided her toward her quarters, just as he had done with me the night before.

A brief, fond appreciation of his sweetness passed through my mind, but the situation at hand promptly chased it away.

I could not stay sitting down with all the thoughts in my head, so I got to my feet and started pacing back and forth across the drawing room. It was jarring to consider how things had developed in such a short time, how clearly proven that damned letter's portents of bizarreness had been. And after everything that had happened heretofore, there was now, of all things, a grave robbery!

I had been at Bristlewood Manor for only four days, and already my life had become an erotic Gothic novel (a comment I make knowing full well that the cynical readers who misinterpret my story as fiction will think it a droll bit of irony).

The moment Mr. Fairfield stepped foot in the drawing room again, I set in on him, quite forgetting the etiquette our roles required. "How could you sit there and say we should just do nothing? That was unthinkable! Grave robbery is a serious offense, you know, and you —"

"Please, Mr. Hayward, take a breath, I beg of you," said Mr. Fairfield calmly and seemingly not affronted by my lack of propriety. "Mrs. Hawthorne is a half-cracked old woman, and I, for one, am certain she did not see what she believed she saw. For someone of her age and health, a walk that long would have taken so much out of her, so I can hardly blame her for any flights of fancy. And the strain of racing all the way back here, already under one wrong impression of the circumstances, would have no doubt been a crucible for all sorts of ridiculous ideas. There is nothing to do but pity her and wish her well in her recovery."

"But what if she's telling the truth?" I asked, moderating my tone when what I really wanted to do was yell.

"I intend to not find out," he replied matter-of-factly. He brushed past me and sat down on the sofa

I turned around to gape at him. "What?" I cried, astonished and dismayed at his detachment.

"You must understand, Mr. Hayward," explained Mr. Fairfield, "the immense pain that my mother's death still causes me. To this day, I have yet to visit her grave, because the torture of it would be too much to bear. I might very well die of sorrow if I went to see her burial place for the first time, only to find her body had been snatched. You must know, Mr. Hayward, I have learned from life that there are, in fact, some pains that can be avoided simply by ignoring them."

"But surely you think the grave robber ought to be brought to justice?" I argued.

Mr. Fairfield nodded stolidly. "*If* there is one, then I do think so, and I certainly hope he is. But the odds of it, frankly, are not in my favor. And if he is caught, so what? My mother will still be dead, and her body will still be lifeless, even if they do manage to find it and put it back in the ground. That a man is punished for a crime committed so long after my mother's death will not ease the grief I suffer, and it will not bring her back to life. To involve myself in the headache of addressing this barbarity may seem to be the right thing to do, but it would only bring me more pain."

I sighed, realizing that, although I disagreed with his decided course of action, I could not disagree with his reasoning. Both of my parents still lived, so I could not truly comprehend Mr. Fairfield's feelings. I must trust him to know them himself and to act appropriately in light of them.

"I understand, Mr. Fairfield," I said, now subjugated. "Forgive my tone. It was most imprudent to speak to you that way."

"There is nothing to forgive," said Mr. Fairfield, standing up again and placing a hand on my shoulder. "I appreciate your desire to see justice done. But please, do not let that desire lead you to do anything rash, which I have a mind to think you might. My parents' graves are deep in the woods, and you would never find them before you died of thirst or exposure. In fact, as such, I forbid you to go searching for them. Is that understood?"

"Understood, sir," I answered.

"Very good," he said. "And now, I believe I shall retire to my apartment if you should need me for any reason. Our lesson must have been near its end anyway, and I am much too distracted now to take it up again. Oh, and do tell Mrs. Hawthorne that she doesn't need to worry about bringing me dinner tonight. I have no appetite, what with all the excitement, and she needs to rest to regain her wits and her strength. I can't have her out of commission for too long."

We exchanged nods with one another, and he left my company.

There were two things I found strange in his last bit of speech: first, that he could skip the one meal he took each day without another thought; and second, the phrase "if you should need me for any reason." My understanding was that I was never to go on the second floor, and the one allowance he had made had been for the sake of licentious motives. Here, it seemed he had granted another exemption, and "if you should need me for any reason" sounded like an invitation should my carnal needs arise again.

No, I was probably overthinking that. And besides, the truth was he hadn't summoned me upstairs yesterday to make love in the first place, but rather, to have a private conversation about his mother's journal. The subsequent love-making came about as a result of several missed opportunities on my part to escape before the temptation became too much.

Shoving that aside, I returned my attention to the macabre matter of his mother's missing corpse. I couldn't believe Mrs. Hawthorne had been deceived by her own mind, for she seemed to me rather astute for her age. But I reminded myself that Mr. Fairfield knew her better than I did, having years of acquaintance with her on his side as opposed to my four days of waspish intercourse.

I resented my helplessness in the situation. I wished there had been something I could've done to assist in some way, but what could I do anyway? Mr. Fairfield had forbidden me from looking for the graves, but in all honesty, I was not particularly keen on wandering the dense woods behind Bristlewood Manor, given the circumstances. The grounds often seemed eerie to me, and the prospect of there being a grave robber about didn't make me any more apt to traipse them.

Mr. Fairfield could have done something, though. And while I could fathom his wish to avoid additional grief by becoming embroiled, I still found his commitment to performing no investigation very queer indeed.

That is, until I remembered the mud I'd espied on his hands and clothes the night before. And then I wondered how he could know where his parents' graves were if he'd never visited them before. But did he say he knew where exactly they were or only that they were somewhere in the woods?

I felt sick to my stomach. Something wasn't right.

# CHAPTER FIFTEEN

Early in this text, when I wrote about my first day at Bristlewood Manor, I described how I'd adjured myself to settle in and get used to the "eccentricity" of the place. I allude now to that passage to point out that this situation – with its weird sounds in the night, its grave robbings, its plenitude of past tragedy, its spiritual struggles, its potential secret twin, and, oh yes, its sexual intrigue – was not what I'd had in mind then.

My suspicions about Mr. Fairfield were unnerving, to put it simply, and I didn't much like thinking of them. But I could not stop myself. It seemed too much of a coincidence that Mr. Fairfield would go out in the middle of the night and come back covered in mud the evening before his mother's grave was found empty. And yet, I could not imagine why Mr. Fairfield would do such a monstrous thing as stealing her body. He so dearly loved his mother, and I doubted he could have desecrated her interment so flagitiously. And aside from being a bit quick to anger, he was a placid, tender, and kind man. He could never have behaved in a manner like that.

I wouldn't believe it, and I didn't.

There must have been a reasonable alternative explanation. But as I could not come up with one, I was determined to find it out. As a cover for myself, I made him dinner, although he said he would take no evening meal, and I was incapable of whipping up anything particularly elegant. But naturally, I would need to eat if Mrs. Hawthorne wasn't going to cook, and surely she required nourishment to aid her convalescence. If there was leftover food once she and I had finished, it would have been thoughtless not to offer it to Mr. Fairfield, who had not eaten in twenty-four hours. So what if he'd claimed he had no appetite? That was, no doubt, a charade to protect Mrs. Hawthorne from overexerting herself.

Unlike Mrs. Hawthorne, I ate before serving the master. I fixed a plate for her and left it at her door with a brief explanation and well-wishing. She thanked me genuinely, so I knew she must have been in a bad way.

Then I took Mr. Fairfield's tray upstairs to the prohibited second floor.

"Mr. Fairfield?" I called out as I walked down the hallway toward his bedroom door, where, for some reason, I had assumed he would be.

But instead, a door on the other side of the corridor opened. Mr. Fairfield slipped out and shut the door behind him almost before he'd fully passed through it.

"What are you doing up here?" he asked, looking and sounding almost as if he'd been caught in the act of a crime.

I held up the tray in my hands as he quickly approached me. "I brought you dinner, sir," I explained. "I know you said you would not eat, but I made meals for Mrs. Hawthorne and me. There was extra food after we had taken ours, so I thought I would bring the rest to you."

"Oh," he said, accepting the tray from me with a slight smile and a grateful nod. "That was very kind of you. Thank you."

"I didn't think you truly wanted to go two days between meals," I said. "And besides, after you helped me up to my quarters last night, I figured it was the least I could do. Oh!

That reminds me." I acted as if a thought had just struck me, even though I had planned this scene in advance. "Were your hands dirty last night? There were some brownish stains on my nightclothes when I woke up this morning. I'm hoping that is the explanation because if not, then I've been up to some strange and potentially concerning sleepwalking adventures."

Mr. Fairfield laughed, and he looked so handsome when he did so. I did not bring the thought "into captivity," as the Apostle Paul writes that we ought, and it became a seed planted invisibly in the soil of my consciousness.

"Oh, I'm very sorry about that," he said, looking down at his hands, which were now clean. "As you remember, it rained all afternoon yesterday, so the ground was all mud and sludge. It was probably not the best night to go out for a walk, but I had a great deal weighing on my mind, and moving my feet has always helped me in such times of agitation. Anyway, as you might expect, I lost my footing not once, but twice, and I caught myself with my hands both times. I was a filthy mess by the time I made it back inside."

I smiled back at him, relieved at this explanation, which I bought wholeheartedly. Thank God he hadn't been digging up any graves, I thought, though I knew the likelihood of that being the case was remarkably slim.

If only I could have naturally transitioned into asking him about his clandestine twin. I would have loved to receive a similarly simple elucidation to that question. Instead of that, though, I inquired, "How are you managing with the news of your mother?"

"I have not given it a second thought," he replied. Then, he set the tray on the floor and turned back to me, looking somber. "Listen, before you go, I wanted to apologize to you for ... everything that occurred yesterday. As you know, I do not believe, as you do, that what we did yesterday was wrong, but I do believe it was wrong of me to seduce you like that. And I do believe it was wrong of me to shout at you for your ... negative reaction. I'm very sorry, and I hope you shall forgive me."

I hadn't expected or particularly needed any apology from him, and I had no idea what to say in response. The sin we'd committed, for so I still maintained it was, had been a mutual indiscretion. I didn't hold him at fault for it, for it wasn't my place to do so; he must account for his decisions with his maker, as I must do with mine.

"In truth," I said, "I don't feel it necessary that you should apologize. I made the choice to go to bed with you. You did not exert any mind control over me, nor was I manipulated into doing anything I didn't want to do. If I was seduced, it was only because I find you ... very naturally handsome."

Why did I add that last part? I am afraid, reader, that I still haven't the slightest clue except that that aforementioned seed was now germinating.

Mr. Fairfield blushed at the compliment. "Well, then I thank you for that," he said. "But I must admit I find myself now confused. You say you wanted to do it and that I did not force you. While I am comforted to hear that, I cannot but wonder, then, at the way you recoiled when we had finished."

I sighed and shrugged. "I don't know how to explain it to you, sir. You don't want me to express your father's beliefs on the matter, but, in some way, I hold them too, whether I like it or not. It's not that I admire your father or his actions, for I certainly don't. I think it was reprehensible the way he treated you and your mother. But as to his attitudes toward two men … being together like that … as we were … they did not originate with him, nor are they unique to him. They are the moral values of the majority, I should think. I pray you will not despise me for still clinging to the beliefs that were instilled in me since my birth."

"I do not, nor could I," said Mr. Fairfield, dropping his gaze to the floor. "But even so, it pains me that you are still trapped in such a prison of faith. I know what it is to be in bondage while knowing there is beauty in the world outside. I must think you tasted a bit of that freedom yesterday, before the shackles clamped back on your soul. I only wish you could experience the freedom I have. For you see, if there's a silver lining in the deaths of my mother, my wife, my daughter, and my father, it is that I have found liberation. Not only was I freed from my physical exile when I inherited Bristlewood Manor, but I was also freed from all the attachments of family. Miserable as that latter liberation was, it allowed me to see clearly the gross negligence and cruelty of the divine. With that wisdom, I was freed from the restraints of such an unworthy master. And in the independence of that wisdom, I have started to find beauty. I'm still at the start of that journey, but I'm hopeful. And what a joy it is to be hopeful! I tell you, Edwin, if there is a God, and if he pulls all the strings of history, then he is utterly wicked; and if, upon my death, I am cast off from him forever, then so much the better, for an eternity spent in the presence of such a diabolical deity seems quite like hell to me."

Once more, I was stunned by him. Whatever he lacked in education or *savoir-faire*, he certainly made up for in philosophical profundity.

But it rankled me the way his profane disquisition sounded so logical and coherent. Even convincing. Until meeting Mr. Fairfield, I had never thought to question God's trustworthiness or the rectitude of his laws. It would have struck me as perilously seditious, and I suppose it still did then. And yet, had I not, just the previous night, wept over the way things were? Had I not mourned for the prison of faith, as Mr. Fairfield had put it, into which I'd been born?

"I wish I could believe as you do," I replied after pausing to puzzle over it all for a moment. "Perhaps I will in time, but the very thought of it terrifies me. You say you are hopeful, but I am only fearful. When you came up to my room yesterday, you said you heard me screaming in my sleep. I will now readily own I was having a nightmare, a vivid and gruesome vision of hell. That's what scares me. And I'm so afraid I have irreversibly consigned myself to that fate with what we did yesterday."

Mr. Fairfield placed a consolatory hand on my shoulder. I let it be, for it did, to some degree, console me. "I'm sorry you had to experience that," he said sincerely. "And I'm sorry we are taught to believe that the creator of the universe, who put us here without our consent, will condemn us to hell if we do not conform to his wishes. That we are commanded not to kill or steal or harm is something I can agree with. But it's a terrible shame that we are so cruelly restricted with respect to who and how we love. It makes claims like 'God is love' very difficult for me to accept."

I nodded, finding myself in full agreement with him, sacrilege be damned. After all, I had already committed the sin of lying with another man "as he lieth with a woman," so I didn't think I could sink much deeper than that.

"I wish there was a way to persevere in my faith while pursuing the longings of my heart," I declared, growing suddenly emotional. "But I am stretched between the twain, and each is towing in the opposite direction of the other, each moving with its own motives while I am torn asunder. To relent fully to either would require me to cut off a piece of myself."

The last words blurred my vision with moisture, which watered that sprouting seed. Pardon any specter of melodrama, dear reader, but it's difficult to keep the tears dammed up while allowing a deluge of your innermost emotions to spill forth.

"Then how will you choose?" asked Mr. Fairfield, still gripping my shoulder with his fingers. "It seems that, if you do nothing, you will be ripped in half, while if you make a decision one way or the other, you will only lose one small part of yourself."

"I don't know," I said. "It seems the fear of hell is an inexorable force on me. If only there were a more powerful and irresistible force driving in the other direction, then, perhaps, I could be free of this torment."

"I'm sorry," he repeated. "I wish I could pull you toward me. I must say, I don't merely long for your freedom for your own sake, but for mine too."

I gaped at him, unable to speak.

"If I were a lesser man, I suppose I could coerce you to go to bed with me again," he added with a chuckle.

I didn't see the humor in it, but neither was I offended. Rather, I was inspired, and my tears dried up suddenly. They were no longer needed, for the seed had blossomed, and the fruit had grown; but it was the proverbial evil fruit brought forth by the corrupt tree.

Either I didn't recognize it, or I didn't care.

"But why should you not?" I asked. "You do not cower in the face of eternal torment as I do, and you are a compassionate man. You know what my deepest desires are, and you know that my convictions forestall the fulfillment of those desires. With that awareness, how could you, in good conscience, not … assist me in fulfilling them?"

Mr. Fairfield gawked at me with an eyebrow raised and his forehead furrowed. "Surely you do not mean to imply that I should … compel you … against your will?" he breathed.

I could not contain a smirk. "If I have no choice in the matter, then I can hardly be held responsible for what takes place," I argued. "And you can rest assured in the full knowledge that you will not be forcing me into anything that is not pleasurable to me nor into anything I do not crave in the most profound recesses of my soul."

"Do you really mean that?" he asked with a nervous laugh. "It sounds like a bizarre joke, though I admit it's not one I'd expect you to make."

I shrugged, still grinning. "I am not the master of the house."

Mr. Fairfield straightened and put on a dignified air. "That is true, Mr. Hayward," he said, plucking the fruit from my corrupt tree. "I am the master of Bristlewood Manor. You work for me, and you are only still employed because of my ongoing mercy. And as such, I demand you kiss me."

I did as I was commanded, as there seemed to be no other choice left for me. Leaning in close, I smothered his lips with mine. I didn't want to feel or acknowledge the gratification that kiss brought me, because that would despoil the charade. I had to be impotent and violated, lest I be culpable.

"And, now, I demand that you come with me to my bed," whispered Mr. Fairfield against my lips.

A typical captive or serf doesn't smile at his master's demands, but I did. I couldn't help it.

May God forgive that smile.

Mr. Fairfield followed me to his chamber with his hand on my hip, leaving his dinner tray on the floor in the hall. There was plenty else for him to feast on first.

# CHAPTER SIXTEEN

By the light of an oil lamp amid the oncoming night, Mr. Fairfield grabbed me by the chin with his thumb and forefinger and narrowed the distance between our faces to a few inches. "If you do not do everything I say," he sneered, slipping into his role quite nicely, "you will be summarily dismissed from your post. Is that understood, Edwin?"

His tone and gesture excited me, but I was determined to be convincing as well. "Yes, Mr. Fairfield," I replied with false deference.

"In this room, even though I am the master, I am to be called Halifax," he reminded me. "Is that understood?"

"It is quite well understood, Halifax."

"Very good," he said stiffly. He kissed me and then released my chin with a wink. "Now, take off all of your clothes right here in front of me. And I mean all of them. I want to watch, and I want to see *everything*."

With a nod and ten excited fingers, I pulled off my ascot, coat, and waistcoat, and then my shoes and socks.

"Faster!" barked Halifax. He stood there like a stringent overseer, diligently supervising me and looking as if he might break out a whip if I didn't get a move on.

Startled by his volume, I ripped off my shirt so briskly I thought I heard a stitch or two pop. I shoved down my trousers just as quickly, stepping out of them to present myself entirely nude to the master of Bristlewood Manor, just the way he wanted me. He made no attempt to hide how studiously and libidinously he eyed my body, nor to conceal the way he rubbed the front of his trousers.

Obviously, I was naked, but I felt particularly naked right then, with him fully dressed and me utterly exposed.

I wasn't uncomfortable with that incongruous dynamic, though. Halifax wore a facade of tyranny, but I knew he read my form with sentimental eyes. I felt it like the warm rays of sunlight, and I wanted to bask in the brilliance of his gaze.

But that wasn't how it was to be. I had to succumb to the hyperbolic (at best) profession that I was an unwilling participant in this situation, although the fact that my penis was already as hard as a rolling pin didn't lend much support to my sincerity.

"Lie down on the bed with your prick face up," ordered Halifax, stepping forward to flick my apparatus with his fingers, "and spread out your hands and feet as wide as you can."

I splayed out on the mattress just as he had directed me, my bare, stiff cock reposing unreservedly on my belly. As I strained to ignore my inhibitive thoughts – the ones that claimed I could flee that room without any real consequence from my employer – Halifax retrieved a few of his old shirts from his closet, and then he tied each of my hands and feet to a separate bedpost. Once he'd finished the job, I pulled on the bindings and found I was quite competently restrained. There would be no retreating now. There would neither be any resisting whatever Halifax planned to do to me, although I doubted I would have anyway.

"Now, watch me strip for you, and do not look away, even for a moment, lest you should regret it," he said. "I want you to take in everything."

Halifax set about undressing himself in front of me, taking his time to slowly tantalize me with each centimeter of skin he revealed: shoulders, arms, nipples, navel, toes, ankles, knees, thighs. And, dear reader, I was excessively tantalized by all of it, particularly when he unveiled his erection to me.

Dear God! I had missed that thick stand of his, and I did not mind staring straight at it, though I could have looked away if I had chosen.

Fully nude now, he approached the bed, leering lewdly at my body from my head to the tips of my toes and everywhere in between. With his left hand, he slowly masturbated himself, wantonly drawing his foreskin forward to enshroud his glans and backward to divulge it again. The demonstration had an almost hypnotizing effect on me, and a sudden influx of wetness filled my mouth.

Meanwhile, with his right hand, he grabbed my cock and briskly stroked it, a devilish smile twisting his face.

"You like that, yes?" he asked, but not with curiosity; he was apprising me of my satisfaction by way of a question.

"Yes, sir," I breathed, though I didn't need the guidance. I liked the contact of his palm and fingers very much. There was no refuting that, and I didn't feel a religiously-prompted compulsion to lie about it, either to him or to myself.

"Then let me hear how much you like it," he enjoined in a fierce whisper.

I commenced moaning as he plied my cock, working my long, lax prepuce over my ruby red head. Those bestial noises resonated through the room. They animated him too, as he sped up the pace of his left hand on his prick and fused his harmony with my melody.

All reservations faded away, and only with considerable effort did I remind myself that this wasn't a mutual enterprise. I was entrammeled and helpless, I told myself, and if I were at liberty to escape from his touch, I surely would have. It could not be a lie, per se; nor could it be a truth, for the reality was, I was trapped, and any speculation as to what I would have done if I'd been free to act of my own volition was unprovable in either respect.

Halifax disengaged his hand from my phallus a few minutes later and got up on the bed, straddling me with his legs. He placed his knees in my stretched-out armpits and his ass on my chest, allowing his practically negligible weight to settle down on top of me. Seizing me by the hair, he wrenched up my head and conducted my gaze toward his tumescent penis, which he waggled mesmerizingly in front of my face. Then, with his hips lunged forward, he buffeted the side of my face several times with his cock.

*Slap. Slap. Slap. Slap. Slap.*

My mouth fell open in anticipation of what I knew would come next, and Halifax accommodated my hunger, insinuating himself between my unsealed lips. It afforded me unmitigated felicity to taste his tool again, especially after I had stingingly vowed not to wind up in another similar situation.

But, when I remembered my earlier prediction that I would fall into this temptation again, I reminded myself — even as I ardently consumed him — that it was not my own will to do so; rather, it was a regrettable obligation to eschew his retaliation. I certainly did not use my tongue to tinker with his foreskin for my own personal amusement. Of course not.

"Look at me while you suck my prick," snarled Halifax from above. "And moan real loud so I know that you love it."

I raised my eyes to meet his and started mewling for him as he oscillated his hips. He fixed me with a lecherous glare, no doubt relishing the image of me powerlessly pressed underneath him, his cock encased in my mouth.

I told myself it was an odious and degrading scene, but my twitching phallus confuted the claim. I wanted this. I wanted him.

Halifax rescinded his cock from my lips and released my hair, allowing my head to fall back on the pillow. He nudged his hips further forward and plopped his dangling sack right on my forehead, fastidiously drawing it down my face as if, by doing so, he was applying some sort of ointment to my skin. He stopped with the drooping, precious purse resting on my lips, and I extended my tongue to lap at the sleek, sericeous skin, sniffing and relishing his musty, masculine scent as I did. Then, I separated my jaws and admitted both of his balls into my mouth, dousing them with my saliva.

In that position, I had an impeccable view of his member, and, from below, I happily ogled the way it indicated the ceiling with its modest upward arc.

After a while, he reversed his position so his back was turned to me. His knees remained in my armpits, although they were now opposite of the ones they had been in before. He rested his shins on my shoulders while his feet settled beside my ears. Then he sat his ass back on my head, his crack aligning precisely with the middle of my face.

If he'd snuffed out my life that way, I would've died very happy ... at least until I reached the judgment seat.

"You will lick my hole," decreed Halifax imperiously, although his voice was muffled somewhat by his body, which had completely besieged my head. "You will get it nice and soaked, and your tongue will venture deep inside of it. And you had better make me scream."

I complied enthusiastically, getting straight to work on the cultivation of a pool of saliva in his hole with sopping kisses and trenchant licks. As directed, I imposed my tongue against his tightly puckered sphincter and did not relent in my assault on its resistance. Eventually, it loosened up, and I gained entry through his back door. Halifax warbled as I probed further inside of him, and it was quite an effort to convince myself I did not fancy it.

"Oh, yes, Edwin," he whined feverishly. "Lick my hole. Taste me. Oh God, you are so far in there. Oh! And you like it, too, you filthy slut. Well, guess what? I like it, too. Oh, God! I love it."

I heard Halifax spit, and I understood that he had expectorated on his hand when, a moment later, he wrapped my cock in his wet fingers, making the skin slippery with his froth. I hadn't softened in the least down there, but his fiddling ensured I wouldn't slacken any time soon.

He kept his ass on my face for at least five minutes before he moved again, freeing me from that superb oppression to rearrange his body. I lifted my head to observe what he was up to next.

This time, he hovered on his knees above my crotch, once more flourishing his formidable, pulsating erection for me. But, before sitting down all the way, he took my prick in his hand and pointed it straight up toward him. Then he lowered himself down so my cock bifurcated his ass cheeks and poked directly against his hole. After wiggling his hips a bit, he gave a sharp yelp as his hole suddenly unlocked, and my tool penetrated him an inch or so. With deliberate care and a few pathetic whimpers, he slid down fully onto me, my cock sinking into the essential core of him.

Pausing there, Halifax met my gaze. He no longer had that imposing look of a domineering master, for his blue eyes were wide and his comely features were uncertain. But he didn't pull himself off the pole he had plunged into his own body.

We each took a moment to grow accustomed to this new sensation. For me, it was a warm, tense pressure gripping my member, and it did not matter if I liked it or not because I was tied up and incapable of doing anything about it. But in reality, I found it immaculate. It wasn't just the physical sensation; that, in and of itself, would have been enough. But that it was these intimate parts – my cock and his hole – made it all the more stimulating. And that I was actually inside Halifax, *my* Halifax, ... Dear God. What words could describe the magnitude of that rapturous spiritual inebriation? Indeed, having puzzled over the task for some time now, I must conclude that no such vocabulary exists.

Having grown more comfortable with this foreign object inside him, Halifax started to slowly bob up and down on me, his ass gliding fluidly along my cock with the assistance of our saliva. The guttural bellow I let loose came out of its own accord, as I was so vanquished by delight that I could do no other.

Meanwhile, Halifax issued a high-pitched, almost womanly ululation each time he slammed back down on my erection. I could only imagine what that felt like for him to be shagged like a lady, and in a dark, forbidden part of my mind, I hoped to experience his prick in my hole someday.

He accelerated his bouncing, and in turn, his wailing. He gave the appearance of a man mounted atop a trotting horse – if that man was riding without a stitch on him and his erect phallus was undulating exorbitantly with each step the horse took.

For my part, my tool became so inundated with delectation that I dropped my head back onto the pillow, closed my eyes tight, and opened my mouth so I could freely express my pleasure with boisterous, wordless bluster. If I could not liberate myself from my fetters, I may as well enjoy the experience.

And I enjoyed it immensely.

Halifax's screams became more desperate a few minutes later, and I upheaved my head again to see what was happening. He had commenced masturbating himself as he rode me, and I watched his face contort in gleeful agony. No man, I figured, had ever reached such heights of transcendent ecstasy in contemplation of the divine as those to which I saw Halifax soar right then.

But it soon must have become too much for him, because a few moments later, his cock spouted thick streams of semen onto my chest and face.

However, even though he had already come, he did not stop rocking on my prick, which was as riddled with electric piquancy as it had ever been. Between the sight of his vehement ejaculation and the hot splatter of his sperm on my body, I soon achieved my apex as well, and I discharged inside of him, coating the walls of his asshole with my seed.

"Oh, yes!" cried Halifax, throwing his head back in euphoria as I dripped within him. With my softening penis still lodged inside his hole, he stopped jostling and fell forward onto my chest. He set his head next to mine so we were lying cheek-to-cheek.

# CHAPTER SEVENTEEN

It will not shock any of my readers to learn that the specious pretense of helplessness I had applied to excuse another trick with Halifax did not go unchallenged. As my pupil lay on top of me, and as my bound hands and feet tingled, the accusations of profligacy entered my mind again. However, I defended myself by insisting that my one sin was allowing myself to be leashed to the bed with nothing on. And even then, I had only stripped and gotten on the mattress because I had been threatened with a summary dismissal from my occupation. That kept the thoughts of commination at bay.

For a time.

My limp cock slipped out of Halifax's ass, and that seemed to awaken him. He sat up, smiling at me, and tumbled onto the floor, where he went around untying my limbs. Once they had been freed, I shook them out, and the prickle of returning sensation overwhelmed me for a moment. When I could fully feel my fingers and toes again, I moved to get up and dress.

However, Halifax, who had settled back onto the mattress beside me, caught my upper arm and held me steady. "Don't leave," he said. "I want you to stay with me."

"But surely you must want to have the rest of your night to spend alone," I countered, since he had never sought out any company in the evenings. "You have not even had the chance to touch your meal."

He did not loosen his grip on me. "I have had too much time alone," he whispered affectingly, then he leaned in and kissed me.

Obviously, I should have averted my face from his, but, to be frank, I just didn't want to. And certainly, I shouldn't have responded in kind, which I did, and I even inclined myself further into him. Halifax brought his hand up to caress my cheek and ear. This kiss was not a mere prelude to carnal adventure; it was something more profound, something more meaningful, something more alarming.

I disjoined my lips from his and tried to pull away, but his hand was like a vise on my arm. "Don't leave," he repeated softly but adamantly.

"Halifax, please," I beseeched him. "I am neither your wife nor your valet. I must be allowed to return to my quarters. It is the only proper thing to do."

"No, you certainly must not," he replied. "In fact, I forbid it."

"You forbid it?" I gasped. "Halifax, this game has gone on long enough."

"I do not speak in jest," said Halifax sternly. "If you depart from me tonight, you will find yourself immediately dismissed from Bristlewood Manor."

I gaped at him, unable to interpret his level of earnestness. His blue eyes were steely and demanding, and his tone had been austere.

"Stay," he ordered me again. "You will sleep here with me. I demand it."

I sighed, feeling quite trapped – and not altogether displeased with that. "All right," I yielded. "I will stay."

Halifax grinned at me and released my arm. Then he hopped off the bed and strutted to the bedroom door. I watched the rounded cheeks of his derriere ripple with each step he took and treasured the spectacle. He went into the hall, retrieved his dinner tray, and, as he came back, gave me my first quality display of his flaccid penis, which oscillated resplendently atop his pendulous balls. His foreskin had completely swallowed up his purple glans, leaving a little tunnel at the tip.

I couldn't help thinking he was the most gorgeous man in the world, beautiful from his head to his feet and every centimeter in between.

I didn't feel bad for thinking it either.

"I don't mean to aggravate you," I said after Halifax had taken up his seat on the bed with the tray on his lap, "but might I just go out briefly to put on my nightclothes if I am to sleep here tonight?"

Halifax shook his head. "You will sleep naked," he said around a mouthful of food, patting and rubbing my bare thigh. He gazed unabashedly at my various parts. "As will I. There is no need to hide anything from one another anymore, and I don't want to stop looking at you."

It was disquieting to realize how thrilled I was to hear that. I loved seeing his nude body and was pleased to learn he had no plans to cover it up. And to remain *au naturel* before him stirred me, too; there was something sweet and intimate about being on full display with him outside the context of our love-making.

"Yes, Halifax," I assented, trying to sound disappointed and exploited.

I don't think it was convincing.

"Did you enjoy what we did tonight?" he asked, returning to a conversational tone rather than a commanding one. He genuinely wanted to know my thoughts, it seemed, not as a master, but as a lover.

However, I blushed and said, "You must not ask me that. You will recall that I had no choice in the matter, so my enjoyment of it is of no import whatsoever."

"It is possible to fancy a thing you did not choose to do," he argued courteously.

"Well, that is certainly true, I suppose," I granted. "But I believe that, in this case, it would behoove us both for me to not give my opinion with respect to our ... conjugal activities. I did what I had to do to maintain employment at Bristlewood Manor, and in that regard, I am satisfied."

A shrewd smile spread across Halifax's face, but he did not pursue the subject any further.

And now, reader, I will take a brief interlude to address you. I'm sure you must be wondering if I truly held that I was absolved from any guilt because I had surrendered my self-authority to Halifax under his threat. The answer to that is quite complicated, and it can be reduced to a contest between thought and feeling. For you see, to join with Halifax in sexual confederacy had that ineffable soul-feeling of rightness, as if we had been purposefully created to complement one another physically and spiritually; but conversely, what I knew to be correct was that God had unequivocally proscribed the lying of man with man. However, by altering the logic of the situation, by contending that I could do nothing else but comply with Halifax's demands, even if I was not absolutely sincere in that belief, I had tipped the scales slightly in favor of acting according to that right feeling, thus justifying my behavior, somewhat, in my mind. Perhaps it sounds ridiculous, and I fully concede that it was ridiculous. But those who have been in a similar situation, when your brain and your heart are locked in such a vicious and consequential dispute, will no doubt understand. I make no attempt now to condone nor to condemn my conduct, particularly since my story is far from concluded; but instead, I only mean to elucidate my inner struggle. In return, I simply ask for your forbearance with me as I continue to spin this tale, and I hope that, in the full course of reading it, you will forgive any perceived lack of rationality on my part.

Now, we shall move forward.

"I have not asked you yet how you've liked your time here at Bristlewood Manor," said Halifax, as if he had overlooked some crucial punctilio. "The incidents in this bedroom excluded, of course."

"I have liked it very much," I replied, although that certainly did not encompass the entirety of my experience there.

"I'm afraid, in terms of upkeep, it is not quite up to the standards of your typical great house," said Halifax. "Surely, if you had taken up a tutelage post someplace else, you might have had a much more comfortable arrangement."

"Be that as it may, Bristlewood Manor is a charming place, in its own way," I told him. I didn't know if that was true, considering all the strange events of the past few days, but I hadn't the heart to explain all of my actual impressions. I didn't know if he was self-conscious about the state of his mansion, and I had no desire to find out by exasperating him. "But may I ask," I continued, "why do you only keep

Mrs. Hawthorne for a housekeeper? No doubt you could afford to employ more servants, and no doubt they would have plenty of things to do around here."

Halifax, having finished his dinner, set the tray of empty plates on the floor beside the bed. "I could afford that, indeed," he said, adjusting his genitals and then folding his arms over his chest. "My father left me an enormous fortune when he died, which I must admit was rather surprising, since I had expected him to name as his heir someone he considered much more worthy than me. But when I arrived back at Bristlewood Manor after nearly a fifteen-year absence, I was very much a changed man. There was a full staff then, but I was overwhelmed by the number of people bustling about, wanting to do things for me and poking their noses into my business. I had grown quite accustomed to a more simple life in Antigua, you see. So, I dismissed everyone except my steward and Mrs. Hawthorne, for I needed at least one other person around to keep things from going to complete ruin, and, as a child, she had always been so kind to me."

I found that difficult to accept, but I felt no need to point it out; perhaps Mrs. Hawthorne had a soft side somewhere, though where that was, I shuddered to find out.

"Do you plan to hire more servants eventually?" I asked. "Surely you must at least want a valet or someone to keep the grounds. Or perhaps someone to maintain a carriage for you."

Halifax shrugged his bare shoulders. "I have not thought of it, to be honest. Certainly, as Mrs. Hawthorne continues to age, she will not be able to keep up with everything she does currently. But for now, I am just trying to get my feet underneath me."

"Get your feet underneath you? What do you mean by that?"

"Well, one cannot be the master of a house like Bristlewood Manor if he has not the ability to read or write, nor if he cannot comport himself in a manner fit for the station," he said matter-of-factly. "That is why the first post for which I hired was a private tutor."

"I see. And, forgive any impertinence, but I'm curious: do you plan to remarry and sire an heir to Bristlewood Manor?"

Halifax laughed genuinely, which I had not expected. "No, I should think not," he said. "As I have explained, I dearly loved Virginia, but it was an arduous situation, you understand, given my … preferences … in the bedroom." Here, he reached out and caressed my penis, as if his allusion required any clarification. "And the pain of losing her, and my precious Sophie, was too much to consider ever attempting to marry again. Perhaps I will adopt an heir someday, but producing one myself is unthinkable. The process of it is … disagreeable."

"That is certainly understandable," I commented. "I doubt I shall ever marry either, given my preferences in the bedroom." I returned his caress with one of my own.

His cock twitched under my hand, and he looked at me with his tongue pressed against his upper lip.

But he didn't make any moves toward more sex.

"As it turns out, universally acknowledged as that claimed truth may be, not *every* single man in possession of a good fortune is in want of a wife," he said, grinning as he made a poignant reference to the novel we had used in our reading lessons.

"So, you were paying attention," I said with a chuckle.

"Why, of course!" exclaimed Halifax. "Do you not think I take my education seriously?"

"No, no, I was merely making a joke," I replied. "It is a quip an old teacher of mine used to make whenever a student clearly showed he had learned something. I'm afraid it is not the most sophisticated humor though."

"Well, I'm not the most sophisticated man, so I will forgive it. Because I am … magnanimous." He winked at me to demonstrate his self-satisfaction at remembering the word I'd taught him the day before.

I smiled back at him, the proud teacher of an excellent student. "Très bien!"

"Oh, please, no French yet," he laughed. "At least allow me to become proficient in written English before we move on to any other languages."

"Deal," I said, winking at him.

"I wonder, Edwin, if you might tell me more about yourself," said Halifax, abruptly changing the subject. "I have revealed a great deal to you about my history, almost to the point of embarrassment on some subjects, but I must admit that I know so little about you aside from how your cock tastes and the fact that your father is a clergyman. So tell me: who is Edwin Hayward?"

That was a fair request. I unrolled for him the yarn of my life to that point, outlining the makeup of my family, which included my mother and father, my two elder brothers, and my younger sister. We were a family of middling fortune with only a handful of servants at our disposal. Ours was a generally happy, if strict and religious, home. I received my education via a boys' school during the day until I had attained such an age as to attend college. As the youngest of the three sons, I was tasked with making my own way in the world, though the pursuit of an occupation in the church and the military held no appeal to me, regardless of my parents' encouragement.

I told Halifax about how I had returned to my family's home to work at my old school after college and with the hope of finding a wife. But courtship did not suit me for obvious reasons, nor did teaching so many naughty children, and so I decided to pursue a new undertaking in the form of providing private, in-home education as a tutor.

"So, I advertised my services and received your offer, and that is how I came to be at Bristlewood Manor," I concluded.

"And it is an enormous blessing to me that you did," he remarked. Then, he eyed my bare body up and down, divulging his unspoken meaning, which was that the extent of the enormous blessing passed beyond merely what I put forth as a tutor. "What was it about courting a young lady that did not suit you?"

My cheeks turned crimson at the question, although I knew my explication would be heard by a sympathetic and commiserative audience. "It soon became incontrovertibly evident to me that I would have made a sorry husband. Alas, whatever draws me to other men is not to be found in a lady. You've seen how quickly I become aroused with you, but I could never imagine that happening with a woman. As I courted, I felt neither interest in nor attraction to any of the women with whom I kept company; neither could I foresee either developing through time and proximity. To marry in spite of that cognizance would have been, in my opinion, a gross and uncharitable error."

"Do you find my marriage to Virginia to have been a gross and uncharitable error?" asked Halifax, his tone revealing that he feared I thought less of him for it.

"I am in no position to adjudicate with respect to your past decisions," I said conscientiously, "especially considering the unjust and desperate nature of your situation. You did what was best for you and for the circumstances in which you found yourself."

He appeared pleased and assuaged by that answer. "Well, I suppose it is getting late," he pointed out. "I imagine you must be eager to sleep, though I will probably still be up a while longer. I do not sleep well these days."

A stab of chagrin pierced me at that, and I felt as if I were a child being sent off to bed. True, I probably could have gone right to sleep then, given how poorly I had been able to rest since arriving at Bristlewood Manor, but our confab had been far too agreeable for me to wish for its termination. I rather fancied this private discourse, divorced as it was from our roles of teacher and pupil, employer and employee.

"I don't mind staying up with you," I offered. "I'm not at all tired."

"Are you sure?" asked Halifax. "I wouldn't want you to be left without the rest you require."

"I am quite sure," I replied. "I would not have said so if I were uncertain."

He beamed at me. "Well, if that is the case, then I wonder if we might do something."

"What is it?" I asked with a gulp. I was not in the proper mood then to initiate another round of love-making.

"Would you read my mother's diary to me?" he asked sweetly.

I pray you will overlook the tiredness of the statement "my heart melted," for there is no other way for me to describe what happened within me. My heart melted. That he wanted me to do something so innocent, and that he loved his late mother so ardently, endeared him to me with such fierceness that I nearly kissed him.

But instead of that, I simply said, "It would be my pleasure, Halifax."

Halifax retrieved the diary from a drawer in his bedside table and handed it to me. Holding its leather binding in my hands again spurred a query, one I had not yet thought to pose to him.

"Halifax," I said slowly, running my fingers nervously over the spine, "how did you know I was in possession of your mother's diary?"

He dropped his eyes remorsefully. "I'm ashamed to admit that I trespassed upon your quarters the second night you were here," he confessed. "I don't know what came over me, but I felt this irresistible urge to see you in that … that most vulnerable state of sleep. There is something so captivating to me about a man in the depths of slumber, and of those I have witnessed, you were, by far, the most adorable."

I was simultaneously unnerved by the thought of Halifax watching me sleep and flattered by his admiration of me. It seemed this young man evoked in me a whole range of conflicting thoughts and emotions, no matter what he said or did.

The revelation also dispelled my other, more disturbing hypothesis, which was that his cloistered twin had intruded upon me in my slumber.

"So you did not know previous to that night that I had found your mother's diary?" I asked.

"I didn't even know she had kept a diary," said Halifax. "When I saw it on the table beside your sleeping head, I thought it must have been a book of prayers or psalms. I don't know what possessed me to investigate it further beyond the fact that I was already so taken with you and wanted to know more about you."

"You were taken with me?"

Halifax nodded. "I was quite taken from the moment I first saw you. It seemed a significant reversal of my fate to have had the good luck of hiring such a handsome man as a tutor, although I never dreamed we would end up naked in bed together. But that is not to say I'm not incredibly pleased to have found ourselves here."

I turned away from him, my face reddening, unsure of how to handle his praise. "That is very kind of you to say."

"And what was your first impression of me?" he asked.

"Please, Halifax, do not make me —" I argued, but he cut me off.

"I demand that you tell me," he said, reaching out and stroking my chest with his finger.

I sighed in another acknowledgment of defeat while at the same time gasping at his touch. "Two days ago, when you came into the drawing room and I saw you for the first time, I was immediately struck by your beauty," I said, incredulous that I was even saying the words aloud. Going to bed together was one thing, but verbally expressing an admiration beyond mere lust was quite another. "Although you were clearly in need of some … improved hygiene practices, I was still quite attracted to you. When you asked me to stay with you while you bathed, I longed to do so with every fiber of my being. I very badly wanted to see how you looked … in the bath. It may not surprise you to learn that I'm quite fond of the sight of a naked man, and that I longed to see you like that."

"So why didn't you stay?" he inquired with a sideways cock of his head. "I certainly wouldn't have minded you ogling me."

"Because I … I was afraid."

"Afraid of what?"

"I was afraid that I would stare at you too long, or that I would become aroused," I said, feeling my face flush red. "I had no reason to suspect that you would have been … understanding, and I feared you would find me out for being a …"

My words trailed off. I did not know what terminology I ought to use to describe what I was aside from "reprobate sinner" or "unnatural cur," neither of which would have garnered a positive reaction from Halifax.

But Halifax took my meaning, even without the words.

He reached around and clasped me by my far shoulder, drawing me close and resting his forehead against my temple. "I'm sorry the world has made you so afraid," he whispered tenderly. "You deserve better than that, and I hope you'll come to accept that someday."

I turned my head to look at him, and somehow, we ended up with our lips crammed together again. I don't know how much blame to lay at my own feet for its initiation, but I was undeniably guilty of not severing it. However, any lingering intrusive, persecutory thoughts faded away with that kiss, for while I was locked in it, I felt as safe as I had ever been.

It was Halifax who ended the kiss, though he kept his arm wrapped around me. With that hand, he pulled me until I fell upon his chest. Then he held me with both arms and rested his chin on the top of my head, breathing in my hair through his nose.

We lay like that for a long time, neither of us saying a word. There was no need for us to speak. Although our experiences in life had been vastly different, we had both suffered under the weight of our atypical predispositions, and we had found in each other another person who could understand and commiserate. The warmth of his body was like a salve on my soul, and I soaked in the succor of his presence and proximity, listening to his beating heart and respiring lungs.

From birth, I'd been indoctrinated with the teaching that God loved me, and perhaps I'd believed that when I was a very small boy. But that awful awakening to the fact of my preference for my own sex, and the knowledge of God's law against that, had irremediably shattered that conviction. The love of God, professed as it was for all sinners, was suddenly inaccessible to me. Or so it had seemed. Although I did my best to avoid temptation and put my faith in the name of Christ for the justification of my many egregious sins, I had never felt loved by him; I had never felt saved by him; I had never felt "the peace of God, which passeth all understanding."

I had never felt anything like it, at least, until that night, when I reclined in Halifax's arms. There, I felt loved. There, I felt saved. There, I felt at peace. I couldn't imagine a more divine embrace than his, nor could I fathom how anyone would find this unholy if an ancient book hadn't told them to do so.

Our shared nudity at that moment was no longer merely prurient; it had become an expression of mutual affinity and mutual recognition, an intimacy beyond anything I'd ever thought possible. I'd hidden myself for so long, but with Halifax, I'd not only bared my body, but I'd bared my soul. There was a faint undertone of shame, of course, but the sweeping resonance was one of relief and tranquility.

Over time, Halifax's breathing deepened and slowed. I turned my head to find that he had fallen asleep, his countenance resting in perfect serenity and contentment. I did not repress my smile as I observed him, appreciating his earlier claim about the charm of a slumbering man. And indeed, Halifax must have been the most beautiful sleeper I had ever seen. I could have watched him sleep all night.

But I wanted to rest too, and I expected to sleep very well wrapped in his arms.

Carefully, so as not to wake him, I reached out to set the unread diary on the table and extinguish the oil lamp. Now awash in darkness, I resettled my head on his bare, thin, hairless chest and fell asleep, as if his body were the most comfortable pillow in the world.

# CHAPTER EIGHTEEN

"Ahh – ahh – ahh – ahh – ahh – ahh – ahh – ahh – ahh – ahh –."

I bolted upright in bed with my heart hammering, the scene having become well-practiced by this point, the fourth straight night of its performance. But, by the scant, blue moonlight, I perceived that the setting was different from all the others: I was not in my cramped quarters on the third floor but in Halifax's bedroom on the second.

That was new and confusing

Turning toward the spot where Halifax had nodded off earlier, there was just enough light for me to see that he was still there, still fast asleep, neither the source of nor bothered by the screaming.

That could only mean one thing.

The twin, or whoever it was, had emerged and taken center stage.

"Halifax?" I whispered.

He did not stir. Perhaps that was for the best. He ought to stay asleep until I'd figured out what was going on.

Trembling less from terror and more from investigative zeal, I rolled over in bed, swung out my legs, and set my feet silently on the floor. I tiptoed around the bed to the bedside table, where I took up the oil lamp. After subtly igniting it, I ensured that the nude body still in the bed actually belonged to Halifax.

It did, and thankfully, he did not rouse itself with the sudden light.

There was no longer any doubt now: there was someone else in the house, the intelligence of whose presence Halifax had, for some reason, kept from me. I couldn't help feeling somewhat deceived and betrayed, although I told myself there must have been a good reason for it. I had come to trust Halifax, and I wouldn't let myself believe he'd do anything nefarious.

I briefly considered at least putting on my pants before stepping out of the room, but I feared that might have roused Halifax, and I did not want him to awaken until I had pried into the sounds for myself. If he had not disclosed this other resident of Bristlewood Manor to me before, I suspected he would have tried to keep me from discovering the truth now.

And besides, whoever was in the other room would indubitably have been in a much more compromising situation than I was.

So, as naked as the day I was born, I slipped out of the bedchamber and passed through the corridor toward the room with the mirror, from whence the wails quite obviously issued. Upon reaching the closed door, I noiselessly set down the oil lamp and paused there for a moment, listening.

"Ahh – ahh – ahh – ahh – ahh – ahh – ahh – ahh – ahh –ahh –."

The cries were identical to those Halifax had produced the night I had watched him from that exact spot, and I marveled at how two people could sound so alike while performing an intimate action like that. It didn't seem possible that would have been a natural development, but any other explanation smacked of something quite uncouth.

And, I must say, I found it a bit exciting too.

I took a deep breath to collect myself, knowing that the moment I peered inside that room, I could no longer deny what was in there, and something would inevitably be different.

Additionally, I admit the invigorating thought briefly crossed my mind that I was probably about to witness another naked man frigging himself. The consequences of it would be what they would be, but it would still be thrilling.

I wrapped my quivering fingers around the knob, turned it inaudibly, and opened the door just a crack.

No one was there.

Or rather, I didn't *see* anyone in the moonlight. The chair was empty, and no candles coruscated on the floor.

And the screaming had abruptly stopped.

Picking up the oil lamp, I threw open the door and stomped inside. But even with a full view and better lighting, there was still no one to be found. Neither were there any other doors through which one could escape, nor any furniture aside from the chair and the mirror behind which one could hide. The window, I checked, was securely closed.

"Sinnersinnersinnersinner!"

I spun on my heel, looking for the person who had spoken. But, of course, I didn't see anyone. There was no one. The voice, like the orgasmic yelling, was in my head. No wonder Halifax had slept through it.

There was no twin. There was only my own madness and my desperate attempts to explain it away.

It was only me.

"Sinnersinnersinnersinner!"

"No!" I cried out against the allegation. "Leave me alone! Leave me alone!"

This couldn't be. Not after the evening I'd shared with Halifax. Not after the peace I'd found in his arms.

But it was a fruitless endeavor to resist. That peace had only been a brief respite, the like of which I would never find in hell. And that's exactly where I was headed. There was no denying the truth about what I was, and that simple, pithy phrase captured it so well.

"Sinnersinnersinnersinner!"

"Sinnersinnersinnersinner!"

"Sinnersinnersinnersinner!"

Tears blurred my vision, and ghosts danced before me, each of them denouncing me for my wickedness with pointing fingers.

"Sinnersinnersinnersinner!"

The spectral figures came closer, their hands outstretched and preparing to drag me down to my eternal fate.

Wordless, tortured screams burst from my throat. Glass shattered somewhere. I tried to move away from those phantoms, but I fell backward. I did not feel myself land.

Fire blazed all around me.

I was already here. I was in hell.

My new forever home.

"Sinnersinnersinnersinner!"

The dream I'd had yesterday was wrong, it seemed. I did have someone assigned to torture me in the underworld: Mr. William Fairfield.

And he was doing a masterful job of it.

"Sinnersinnersinnersinner!"

I shrieked for mercy. But the time for mercy had long since passed.

And besides, I already knew there was no mercy for someone like me.

"Sinnersinnersinnersinner!"

I might as well get comfortable with the flames and the screeching. It was going to be like this for eternity, after all.

"Sinnersinnersinnersinner!"

"Sinnersinnersinnersinner!"

"Sinnersinnersinnersinner!"

"Edwin!"

"Sinnersinnersinnersinner!"

"Edwin!"

# CHAPTER NINETEEN

Halifax was shaking me out of my stupor.

The flames and the ghosts were suddenly gone, and the haunting indictments were now muted. Every horror had dissipated in a moment as if they had never been at all. There was only Halifax – beautiful, naked Halifax – squatting at my side and gripping me by the shoulders.

I, meanwhile, lay knackered on the floor, my face drenched with tears and sweat and mucus.

There was a faint, burnt smell somewhere in the room. The fire, at least, must have been real, or else I was still experiencing the vestiges of an olfactory hallucination.

"Halifax," I breathed with recognition.

"My God!" he cried, a look of relief rushing over his face. "My God! Edwin? Are you all right? What in the blue blazes happened in here?"

"I do not–, I do not know," I sputtered, my throat raw and my mind a nebulous cloud of confusion.

"My God," he moaned again, sitting me up and clutching me to his body. His hands slipped over my sweaty skin. "You had me terrified, Edwin. I woke up to the sound of someone screaming his head off, and I saw that you were not in bed. I followed the noise and found you in here writhing on the floor, yelling like you were in some awful trance. And the rug was on fire and the oil lamp crushed into a thousand pieces! Thankfully, I was able to easily smother the fire with one of the curtains, and there was no further damage. But what about you? Have you been burned or cut?"

"I don't think so," I said.

But what on earth was he even talking about? It felt like I should have known, but everything was so hazy.

"I'm going to carry you back to bed," he said sedulously. "I have another oil lamp in the room, and then I can check to make sure you have not been injured."

I was incapable of arguing with him, not understanding why he should – nor why he shouldn't – take me to bed. It was just a thing that was going to happen.

With strength that surprised me later, but not at the time, Halifax lifted me in his arms, carefully picked his steps to avoid stepping on the broken glass of the oil lamp with his bare feet, and ferried me back to his bedroom, where he scrupulously deposited me on the mattress. He stepped away to ignite a new oil lamp and then came back over to the bed. Holding it in his hand, he used its light to inspect the front of my body for lacerations or scald marks. Then he rolled me over and did the same with the flip side, scrutinizing in particular the soles of my feet.

This was not a sensuous examination, dear reader, but a frantic one.

When Halifax was content that I had not been physically harmed, he set the oil lamp on the bedside table and heaved an enormous sigh.

"What the devil happened in there, Edwin?" he asked again, still standing beside me. "I must admit I am quite flummoxed!"

"The devil," I repeated automatically, my voice ragged and feeble.

"What?" gasped Halifax.

"I think I saw the devil," I whispered. "No, no, wait; it wasn't the devil. Not really. It was ... It was ... your father."

"But Edwin, my father has been dead for more than a year," he said soothingly, brushing my sweaty hair off my forehead. "You must have been sleepwalking and having a nightmare."

"No!" I bellowed, sitting up suddenly and grasping Halifax's arm.

He gaped at me with wide eyes. "Edwin, you are frightening me," he said in a quivering voice.

"I am frightened, too," I replied, taking a sedative breath and releasing his arm.

Halifax pushed me down until I was reposed on the pillow again. "Just relax now," he cooed like a mother comforting a child awakened by a bad dream. "You're safe here with me. Nothing is going to hurt you."

Then he got in bed on his side next to me, wrapped me in his arms, and gave me a long, affectionate kiss on the cheek.

Every muscle in my body slackened as he held me close. He had such a powerful effect on me. But when my mind had calmed itself too, the details of my ordeal flooded back. I closed my eyes and began to weep quietly.

It was all so terrible to recall, and I feared I would never escape the incipient insanity. Yes, I felt safe in Edwin's arms right then, but I had felt that way earlier too.

Halifax caressed my cheek with his fingers. "What is it, Edwin?"

"I was so scared," I sobbed. "I don't know what is happening to me."

"What do you mean?" he asked gently.

"I have been hearing things that are not there. Tonight, I saw things that could not have been there. I fear I'm going mad."

His embrace tightened, and his thumb lightly stroked my shoulder. "But why would you be going mad? You are young and healthy. You are intelligent and strong."

I sniffled. "I … I believe God is punishing me for my sins."

"But Edwin, we live in a modern, scientific age," he scolded softly. "We know madness has natural causes, not supernatural ones. I'm certain God isn't punishing you. But how long have you been hearing things that are not there?"

"Since yesterday," I replied. "After we…" My voice trailed off. I couldn't say it.

"Fell into amorous congress?" offered Halifax.

"Yes," I said with a bitter laugh at his word choice.

My tears had mercifully stopped. Talking with him seemed to assuage every infirmity.

"What is it that you hear?" he asked.

"There is a man's voice, accusing me of being a sinner," I explained. "I heard it first yesterday while I was praying for forgiveness in my quarters upstairs after going to bed with you. And then I heard it again tonight."

"Whose voice is it? Do you recognize it?"

"Your father's," I said bluntly.

"My father's?" Halifax sounded so bewildered that I wondered if he thought I was making all of this up. "But it's impossible that you would have ever heard my father's voice before. You could not know how he sounds. That is, unless there's something you haven't told me."

"No, I'd never heard his voice before yesterday, and I have no real reason to believe it's him," I confirmed. "But somehow I know it is his voice. I *know* it is."

He nodded, accepting – if not wholly believing or understanding – my claim. "Is that what woke you up tonight?"

"No. The screaming woke me up."

"The screaming?" he asked. "What screaming?"

"It was this awful din," I said. "It sounds exactly like you did that night I saw you ... tossing off in front of the mirror. I heard it again last night, and I simply thought you were at it once again. That's why I went downstairs, where you eventually found me. But then you came in from outside, and I realized it could not have been you making all that racket. And that was why I nearly fainted. I was so shocked and confused. I couldn't wrap my mind around it, but I didn't think I was mad. Not then, at least."

"And then, you heard it again tonight," he inferred solemnly and sagaciously.

"Right. So I got up to see who it was, since it was evident it wasn't you, but there was no one there," I said, recalling the memory with a shudder, although it somehow felt so long ago. "I was so perplexed and horrified, thinking that it was all impossible. Then, I heard your father again. And I saw these…things. Ghosts or something. I don't know. I guess I collapsed and dropped the oil lamp, which caught the rug on fire. I saw that, too, and I believed I had fallen into hell."

"My God," muttered Halifax, giving me another kiss on the cheek. "That sounds awful. I am so, so sorry. I wish you would have woken me up when you first heard it. Are you hearing anything now?"

I shook my head. "It all went away when you came in and started shaking me. I haven't experienced any delusions when I am with you. Or at least not when you've been awake."

"Then you must not leave me!" he exclaimed, hooking his leg around both of mine to further restrain me to the bed. "I forbid it. And I must never sleep again."

"I don't think it's possible for you to never sleep again, but I admit I don't want to leave you," I said, turning my head toward him so our noses were pressed against one another. "But I'm afraid to stay with you."

Halifax gazed at me sadly. "Let me take your fear from you," he said. "Let me rescue you from all those awful beliefs with which you've been brainwashed."

"You already do," I replied. "I feel no dread when I am with you. Not anymore."

"I'm glad," he whispered. With a slight smile, he planted his hand on my cheek. Then, he closed his eyes and adhered his lips to mine.

I accepted the kiss enthusiastically, rolling over onto my side like him so we were front-to-front. My tongue quickly found its way to his, and what had begun as a condolent gesture soon became something much more. It seemed as if it could not have been otherwise, and I needed neither restraints nor excuses nor any other contrivances to pursue what was to follow.

# CHAPTER TWENTY

Despite the night's somber atmosphere, both of our pricks sprung to attention instantaneously. We passed saliva back and forth with our lips and tongues as lust overtook us. I cannot speak for him, but for my part, something about his insistence on our remaining together in spite of my delirious fits filled me with so much longing for him. And somehow, I had come to believe that, if only I had him there with me, I could face my fears directly and be quite all right.

Instead of fighting the ghosts with rote prayer and righteous behavior, I gave in to my desire for him completely.

I realized then that it was, in fact, much more than a desire. It was a need. I *needed* Halifax.

My fingers scrambled frenetically for his rigid cock, and I discovered a great comfort when I found it. His penis felt so perfect in my grip, as if my hands had been specifically designed to clasp its length and girth. I frigged him zestfully, focusing my touch on his glans and foreskin. He poured blissful moans into my mouth as I did.

"I presume I do not need to tie you up this time?" he asked between my ravenous kisses.

"No, no, no," I said, panting from hankering and limited airflow. "I want this with every fiber of my being. I want *you* with every fiber of my being, Halifax."

"I want you, too, Edwin," he replied rapaciously as I moved on to kissing his neck. "Oh, God! I want you so bad."

I rolled him onto his back to turn his member toward the ceiling. Meanwhile, I stayed on my side next to him, shifting my mouth from his lips and neck to suck and bite his earlobes and his collarbone.

God, I loved how his body tasted. It was better than I'd dared imagine the first day I saw him.

I burnished his stout erection with my right hand and flicked his distended nipples with my left. Halifax's groans turned to high-pitched cries when I then took those masculine teats in my mouth, suckling at his flat bosom like a hoggish infant.

But after a few minutes like that, he suddenly caught my hand with his and pulled it away from his penis. "Slow down, slow down, I don't want to come so soon," he explained breathlessly. I looked up at him with his entire areola engulfed in my mouth. "You toss me off so well, my dear, but please, have mercy. Let my prick have a bit of a rest."

"All right," I said disappointedly. "But only for a little while. I can only leave it be for so long."

Halifax shifted as if he were going to focus on pleasuring me now, but I pushed him down to the mattress again. I was not done with him yet.

He had bewitched me with his doting care so much that my singular ambition was now to intimately indulge him in every part and in every way. My erotic craving for him had burgeoned far beyond what I had known on any occasion before, and, as if in open defiance of the phantoms that plagued me, I endeavored to slake my all-consuming thirst for his hallowed body. I did not care how libertine that would require me to be. I would do what I had to do, and I would do it with joy.

I had become a monster of lust, but rather than make me feel ashamed, the thought just made me harder.

But as I wantonly surveyed his body, I realized there were still so many areas of him I had not tasted yet. So, heaving myself up to my knees, I bent over and began to kiss, lick, and suction his hips, the pit between his scrotum and his thighs, and the full length of his legs until I arrived at his feet.

Stretching out my body on my stomach – which allowed Halifax to reach out and grope my ass cheeks – I took his lean right foot in both hands and pecked my lips all over the top and all over the sole. Then, I pulled his long, knobby big toe into my mouth, giving it all the same greedy attention I had given his prick during our previous liaisons. I didn't know what to expect from the act, but it was a stupendous thrill. I thoroughly drenched that digit before moving on to the next knuckly toe and then the next and then the next and then the next. I reduplicated the same rigmarole on his left foot, this time adding some tongue to his sole.

This whole episode was, of course, quite deviant from the sexual standards of our society and even from any of my own previous, private sexual fantasies. But there was something about imbibing his bare toes that felt scrumptiously aberrant to me, and it made me ooze pre-ejaculate on the sheets before my cock had even been touched. Licking anyone else's feet would have nauseated me, but somehow, Halifax's feet were somehow sacred. It didn't matter to me where they had been since the last time he had washed them; they were a part of him, and since I could not get enough of him, I could not get enough of them.

Meanwhile, as the way I had sprawled out had brought my feet right next to Halifax's face, he had moved from my ass and begun to retaliate on my feet, first by massaging each with his silky, strong hands, and then by greedily bathing my soles with his tongue. At first, I suspected he had only taken up my feet out of an obligation of reciprocity, but the way he so rapturously vocalized while licking me between my toes as if he were sampling a sumptuous dessert clearly indicated otherwise.

That only made me wish to do more ribald things to him, but before I could switch up my tasks, Halifax said, "Stand up, Edwin. I want to suck your beautiful prick on my knees like a goddamn whore."

As much as I yearned to keep pleasuring him like that, this new prospect was so tempting that it was impossible for me to rebuff it. And besides, even if I wasn't directly stimulating him, I knew well enough that he would still thoroughly enjoy stuffing my cock in his mouth. If that was what he craved, I could not, in good conscience, withhold it from him. All I cared about was his delight, and it was quite convenient that what delighted him was orally goading me.

So I rolled out of bed and onto the floor. Proudly, I rose to my full height in front of him. Looking down, I saw that my cock was as rigid as it had ever been. I did not deny myself a few self-indulgent strokes of it, which I performed while staring fiendishly at him.

"My God!" said Halifax from the bed, where he lightly teased the tip of his own stand. "Edwin, my dear, you are so damn beautiful. Some day, I want to just sit and watch you toss off. But not tonight. Tonight, I want to suck your prick until you come in my mouth."

I nearly spent right then.

With the concupiscent look of a savage predator, Halifax crawled off the bed and right up to me like one of those big cats from Africa or Asia. Settling himself on his knees between my feet, he ogled up at my protuberant penis from beneath, smirking nefariously.

I wagged my cock and jiggled my balls in front of his face for his unsavory amusement – and for mine. Then, after smacking his face with my adamantine tool, I said, "Suck my prick, you goddamn whore."

"Yes, sir," he replied keenly.

Rising up off his heels with his jaw dropped wide, Halifax slowly and sensually welcomed my phallus into his mouth, maintaining eye contact with me the whole time.

"Ohhhh!" I droned as he slid his wet lips and tongue along my cock, tickling every nerve until he buried his nose in my pubic hair and gagged. "Bloody hell!"

After taking my prick as far down his throat as he could, he inaugurated a brisk pattern of lurching his head backward and forward, and I clutched his hair in my hand to ensure that he kept it up. His captivating blue eyes sparkled joyfully as he gorged himself on my solid priapus, and I loved watching my pasty, white trunk continuously glide in and out of his drooling maw. With his left hand, he fondled my tight sack and its stones, and with the other, he ruthlessly masturbated himself.

The sheer sensuality of the whole arrangement was nearly overwhelming.

"Oh, Christ!" I grunted, the blasphemous oath slipping out before I could stop it. But I hardly even noticed it with all the galvanizing currents coursing through my whole body.

And anyway, it could not have been any more sinful than what I added. “Eat my prick, boy. Eat it so good. Make me come, you goddamn whore.”

“Mmm,” he replied with phenomenal wisdom and perspicacity. He did exactly as he was told, and he did it so well.

Then a new idea promptly came to me. I placed my hands on his shoulders to steady myself, lifted up my right foot, and groped his groin with my sole. He moved his hand out of the way, letting me freely rub him all over the underside of his cock. After also polishing the top of his prick and his balls, I lubricated myself with the clear fluid that burbled up from his piss slit and gripped his purple head with my big and second toes, pointedly stimulating him there. That made him whimper around my tool, which was still deep in his mouth.

But I could only maintain my balance in that position for a short time. When I had to let go of his phallus and plant my foot again, I shoved him to the ground. I lay down beside him, positioning myself so my face was in front of his crotch and my crotch was in front of his face.

There was no need to explain to him what we were going to do; everyone in that situation understands it implicitly, right, dear reader?

Well, anyway, without a word, we introduced each other’s penises to the backs of our throats, muffling our spirited groans with the other man’s prick.

Somehow, in the span of just a few hours and after a spat of sleep and terror, I had already forgotten how delicious his cock tasted on my tongue, especially with his dribbling antecedent juices providing an additional salty flavor.

Although I was in quite an altered state of consciousness right then, I knew I would never live a happy day if I did not suck his prick at some point during that twenty-four-hour period. I also realized that every meal I ate would thenceforth be ruined in comparison with the sweetness of his nether parts.

Halifax somehow, by some strange turn of events, had become my everything, and my primary objective had become knowing and pleasing his body as much as possible.

I took his cock out of my mouth, then pinched his foreskin with the thumbs and forefingers of both hands. Pulling the prepuce out and up, I stuffed my tongue into the pocket I had created and churned against his head directly. A little pond of saliva and pre-come formed therein, and Halifax growled, "Oh, Christ! Holy God!"

As piqued as we were, fate had determined we were not to last much longer. Halifax spent first, and I just managed to get his prick back into my mouth before he blasted his steamy seed down my throat. Those heavenly globules of sperm so comprehensively satiated my gluttony that I ejaculated on his tongue and teeth moments later.

Without stopping to rest, I immediately squirmed my way over to him. We kissed fervidly, exchanging one another's seminal fluids between our mouths. Had I not already come twice that night, I probably would have gotten erect all over again. Our semen had coalesced into a toothsome concoction fit for the gods.

But we did not go another round then as exhaustion soon overcame us. After all, it was the middle of the night, and we had each been awakened in a brusque and terrifying manner. How foreign and far away that all seemed now. The only thing on my mind was Halifax and everything I felt for him, and, in light of that, the memory of the night's earlier trepidation quickly faded away.

We got back into bed and kissed on the lips again before lying down to resume our sleep. I held him this time, my naked front pressed up against his naked back. His plump ass provided an excellent cushion for my cock.

As soon as Halifax put out the light, I nibbled his ear, and my hand traveled down his belly to his shriveled penis.

"Not again, Edwin," said Halifax with a giggle as he tried perfunctorily to shake me off of him. "Not tonight. I want to go to sleep now."

"Oh, relax, I'm just fidgeting with it," I told him as I slipped my finger inside his foreskin and spiraled it around the head. Having been thoroughly exercised, he did not get hard, but that did not matter to me. I just loved to touch him there, to clutch his treasured tool, to revel in the mindful awareness that I was the only one holding it. "It helps me fall asleep."

That claim turned out to be quite true. We were both unconscious within the minute, our breaths turning protracted, profound, and peaceful. As terrible of a day as it had been – complete with an alleged grave robbery and a confirmed mental breakdown – I may have never in my life fallen asleep so content as I did that night, with Halifax's flaccid cock gripped in my hand.

# CHAPTER TWENTY-ONE

I slept all the way until morning.

When I awoke, I was fully aware that I was going mad and falling in love at the same time. While those two experiences are not altogether dissimilar, having them both simultaneously left me, needless to say, nonplussed. How is anyone expected to effectively organize his thoughts in that case?

Thankfully, there had been no more hysterics during the night, and I had not so much as dreamed – or, at least, not that I remembered. And the type of dream about which I was concerned was the vivid, grotesque type that we all tend to remember upon waking, and so, therefore, there may as well have been no dreams. That was surprising, all things considered, but I did not grumble against it. I simply hoped this would be the new status quo, although even that felt quite naive.

Halifax was still fast asleep, lying on his back with his hands cast above his head, exposing his hairy armpits. His face was slightly skewed toward me and lit up by the morning sunlight, which could only make me smile joyfully. His dark eyebrows were furrowed in the effort of slumber, and his brown hair was splayed out on the pillow. His partially erect penis lay flipped up on his belly.

I stared at him for a long time, listening to his breathing, reflecting on my relationship with him, stroking his bare foot with mine, and fondling his cock and balls with my hand.

Do you yet comprehend my complex sentiments for him, dear reader, or must I delineate them for you? I ask only because I am reluctant to offer a full explanation, worried as I am that it would sound quite paradoxical and nonsensical. Such is often the case when one dares to put words to the vagaries of the heart. Nevertheless, I shall attempt it.

I did not deceive myself as to the immorality of my current affiliation with Halifax; that was as manifest to me as was my own name. And yes, I did feel some proportion of culpability, particularly as it related to those deeds executed on my own initiative. But the potency of that guilt and shame was substantially muted by Halifax's propinquity; when he enveloped me in his arms or vice versa, any mindfulness of our malfeasance simply did not matter as much as it would have otherwise. I was, at once, aware that I should have been sickened by my actions and that I was impervious to that very awareness. I had a sense of invulnerability in his presence, both from the ghosts that haunted me and from the consequences that doubtless awaited me in the future.

It was a mad love that seemed to stave off madness.

As I watched him sleep so pacifically, I could not avoid pondering that maybe my presence was a boon to him too. One of the first things I'd noticed about him that first day was how exhausted he'd appeared, and he'd confessed to me that he was not adept at sleeping. And yet, here he was, resting like a baby. Could I really have been so evil if I could help him sleep in that deep, otherwise unknown way?

Halifax woke up fifteen minutes after I did, and he smiled when he saw me beside him, twiddling his most precious organ. We kissed, and our hands cavorted over each other's still-naked bodies, bringing us both to full erection in mere seconds. We were young enough then to go for a third course in the span of twelve hours, and we availed ourselves of that youthful verve with alacrity. Now that I am much older, I can only marvel at how we were able to do that.

"Can we toss off in front of each other?" asked Halifax between kisses. "I would love to watch how you play with yourself."

"Of course," I obliged gladly, although I would miss the opportunity to touch him further.

He moved to the foot of the bed while I remained at the head, and we spread our legs wide open to flaunt ourselves for one another. We exuberantly tugged on our stiff pricks, both of us putting on a show and enjoying one synchronously. He mesmerized me with the way his drooping balls bounced with each stroke he unleashed on his cock.

I reached my crisis first.

"Oh, Halifax, I'm going to come!" I announced, and Halifax fixated his stare on me as I spewed viscous, white semen all over myself.

"Oh, God!" he cried. "Me too now!" A moment later, he, too, ejaculated on his chest and belly.

We licked one another's bodies clean, and then we crawled back to the head of the bed so that we could hold and be held again. During that time, I could not keep my hands off his penis. I'd become obsessed by the thing.

"We never did get around to reading my mother's journal," observed Halifax, gazing over at the leather book on the bedside table.

"Well, you fell asleep before we could start," I pointed out.

"I did, indeed," he laughed. "I think that must have been the earliest I have fallen asleep in years. And, aside from a brief intermission, I must also say that it was the sweetest night of sleep in my life."

"I cannot tell you how pleased I am to hear that," I replied sincerely, kissing him on the cheek.

"And what of you?" he asked with concern. "How are you this morning?"

"I am magnificent," I said, and then I kissed him again, this time on the mouth. "But I am famished. I ought to get up and see if Mrs. Hawthorne has made anything for breakfast. If I don't, I may starve to death."

"Ah, yes, poor Mrs. Hawthorne," said Halifax affectionately. "I will go downstairs with you and see how she is doing. She had such an awful fright yesterday, and I do so hope that she is all right."

I recalled Mrs. Hawthorne's inconsolable conniption as she reported the (alleged) burglary of Mrs. Amelia's tomb. I also thought back to Halifax's queer decision not to look into it. But this time, I felt less galled by it; that was his business, and it was well beyond the reach of my responsibilities as a mere tutor.

And sexual partner.

"And who knows?" he went on. "Perhaps I shall take a spot of breakfast myself."

"I would certainly like to see you eat more," I told him. "But will she not think it odd when we emerge there together?"

Halifax waved away my unease. "She will not think a thing of it," he said. "Mrs. Hawthorne knows me, and I know her. She is a kind, caring, and understanding soul, and she has no interest in prying into the affairs of others."

I hoped that was true, although my exposure to her did not contribute much proof of that. But in any case, I was thus convinced. After all, Halifax had known her much more intimately and for much more time than I had.

We got out of bed and dressed for the first time in half a day. Our clothes were somewhat wrinkled from having lain in a heap all night, but we had no one to impress besides Mrs. Hawthorne, and she could hardly be accused of being *soignee*. I was sorry to see Halifax stow away his nakedness, particularly in such unshapely attire. I reminded myself to speak with him about visiting a tailor.

Before he got all the way buttoned up, I stuffed my hand down his pants and diddled his cock and his ass. Then, after one more kiss — a short but amorous one — we went out of the bedroom. I did not even think to look askance in the direction of the room where I had nearly come completely unraveled in the night. Not with Halifax's fingers entangled with mine.

Mrs. Hawthorne had, indeed, recovered her spirits enough to make a morning meal, and she was seated at the table, ingesting hers, when we entered. Her eyes went wide when she saw Halifax come in just after me, and she got up forthwith and went straight to him.

"Mr. Fairfield!" she cried, grabbing his hands and holding them to her chin. "I could hardly catch a wink all night. You must tell me, sir: did you investigate the graves? What did you find?"

Halifax kissed her decrepit fingers and gave her a soft smile. "I did," he lied. "Everything was all right and just as it should be. I am concerned that you experienced a horrible hallucination of some sort, no doubt the result of such a lengthy jaunt combined with your grief. Pray, tell me you will not make that long walk out there again."

"But I must pay my respects to the people who kept me employed for so many years!" she argued. "Whatever their faults, Mr. William and Mrs. Amelia did right by me."

"I understand and appreciate your desire to honor the memory of my dear parents," he replied evenly, quite like the master of a large manor – who did not romp about with other men – should. "But I beg of you, please take care of yourself first and foremost. I cannot bear to think of what I would do without you. Promise me you will not return to my parents' graves. Please."

Mrs. Hawthorne dropped her eyes mournfully, but she capitulated. "I promise, Mr. Fairfield," she said quietly and sorrowfully.

"Thank you, my dear, sweet Mrs. Hawthorne," said Halifax, drawing her in close and giving her a kiss on the forehead. "And now, madam, I would like to inquire about breakfast."

"Breakfast?" she repeated with surprise. "But you have never taken breakfast since your return to Bristlewood Manor!"

Halifax grinned at her. "I am considering the adoption of a new habit. I have grown rather thin these last months, and I do not think an extra meal a day would be altogether harmful to me."

"No, indeed, it would not!" she returned with glee. She must have been hectoring him for a while to eat more. "Only give me a few minutes to make up an extra portion. I was not expecting you, but I cannot tell you how pleased I am to have you!"

Halifax spent breakfast telling Mrs. Hawthorne all about his reading lessons and the book we had been working through together. For a change, Mrs. Hawthorne showed actual interest in the subject; it seemed Halifax was exempt from her general misanthropy. Throughout that time, he kept looking at me with a revealing smile, which made me blush to the roots of my hair. If he wasn't careful, Mrs. Hawthorne would begin to suspect something.

Perhaps she already did.

Once we had finished eating, Halifax and I retired to the drawing room. We sat on the same sofa, right next to one another. With the book in his left hand, he placed his right on my thigh.

"Halifax, please," I said, pushing his hand off of me.

With a smile, he removed his hand momentarily and then replaced it directly on my crotch, which he squeezed with his fingers. "What is the problem?" he asked, rubbing me along my shaft.

"This would be one thing in the bedroom," I replied, trying to suppress my own grin, "but it is quite another here in the drawing room. What if Mrs. Hawthorne were to walk in and find us like this?"

"We would hear her coming long before she saw us," said Halifax, continuing to grope me. Then, feeling that I had grown unmistakably hard in my trousers, he added, "You cannot tell me you dislike it."

It became impossible for me to hold back my smirk then. I leaned forward and kissed him, clutching his groin with my hand. He was already stiff, and I slipped my hand inside his trousers to feel him skin-to-skin.

Halifax pulled back from my lips with a gasp when my fingers grabbed his bare cock. "Maybe we should continue this reading lesson upstairs," he suggested.

"That might not be a terrible idea," I said. Then, I kissed him again and compressed his prick once more before getting to my feet.

Halifax carried the book up to his bedroom with him, but once we were safely inside, he set it down and took off all of his clothes. I did the same, and we reunited on the bed, kissing and stroking each other. It took us a while to come, given how active we had been recently, but like valiant heroes, we both pushed through, spending our juices all over each other's bare bodies.

When we finished, we did break open the novel again, but we did not get dressed first and simply enjoyed one another's presence in complete nudity. By then, though, we had thoroughly annihilated sex as a potential distraction.

At least, until that evening, when I again put my cock inside his hole and came there.

# CHAPTER TWENTY-TWO

Two weeks passed.

I hope you will pardon such a leap forward in time, reader, but my tale would have grown quite repetitive and stale if I had insisted on painstakingly detailing every day that elapsed in the interim. I'm sure, though, you understand how much of a relief it was to find some stability at Bristlewood Manor after the way my first few days there went.

However, to placate whatever appetite you may have to know what happened during that fortnight, I shall dedicate a few paragraphs to it and no more.

Halifax kept to his word and ate breakfast with Mrs. Hawthorne and me in the kitchen each morning, although she regularly (if unsuccessfully) adjured him to take it in the dining room like a proper gentleman. He also began to devote some part of every evening downstairs before retiring to his apartment for some time alone, which he spent in what he called his study, that private room from which he'd emerged the night I brought him dinner. After I had passed a few hours reading some delightful novel in the drawing room or taking a walk about the grounds of Bristlewood Manor, I would go up to bed — his bed, I should say — where he would join me shortly thereafter.

That's right: I slept every night with him. During that whole two-week period, I did not doze for a moment in that cramped, third-floor bedroom, and I only left my trunk of belongings up there to maintain appearances. Each evening, upon reconvening in his bedroom, Halifax and I immediately shed all of our clothes and dove headlong into exuberant love-making. It never grew dull. My lust for his body was just as robust as it was the first time; if possible, it may have only augmented with each passing day and each passing orgasm. I never tired of sucking his cock or drubbing his ass, and his enthusiasm for me didn't seem to wane either. I came to know his naked body as well as I knew my own. I could have sketched or sculpted him from memory, and the resemblance would have been uncanny.

Whenever we finally spent, we usually followed with sleep, reading together, conversation, or another round of sexual carousing. But I must say, Halifax was as genuinely invested in his education as he was in advancing our joint sexual acumen, and we spent a great deal of time developing his reading skills while naked in his bed. I found that the best way to assist him was to make him read aloud from our novel of love without being distracted by what my fingers, tongue, or lips were doing to his prick, balls, or hole.

And yes, we did get around to reading his mother's diary. It was an exceptional experience, filled with a mixture of laughter and tears, of fond remembrance and profound sorrow. To be able to share that with Halifax, to be let in on his inner life, was a great honor to me, and one I did not take lightly.

Throughout all that time, I didn't encounter a single recurrence of hysteria or hallucination. There was no screaming, there were no verbalized accusations, there were no nightmares; there was only tranquility, joy, and burgeoning love. I rarely found myself questioning the decency of my association with Halifax, and whenever I did, it was always a brief, fleeting moment. Even in those hours we spent apart, when he went up to his study and I was left alone, I was at peace. These were not times of loneliness for me, but of wonderful solitude before I inevitably rejoined my lover.

My life was as bucolic and jubilant as any portrayed in the "happily-ever-after" epilogue of an idealistic country romance novel.

But it was not to last forever.

The event that ultimately broke up this halcyon routine was the arrival of the post one cloudy, blustery afternoon. I was reading in the drawing room when a letter came for me, as Halifax had retreated to his study a bit earlier than usual to pass some time alone.

Although I'd kept my promise to write to my parents, I had never received any correspondence at Bristlewood Manor until that day, and my first letter was dissatisfactory, to say the least. It was from my father. My mother, he reported to me, had fallen grievously ill a few days prior, and the doctor said her prognosis was not encouraging, which is to say, her death was imminent. He exhorted me to return home at once, while there was still time for me to see her.

Before I had a chance to process the information in any way beyond its practicalities, I leaped to my feet to chase down the postman, Mr. Havisham. It was not a difficult feat, as his coach was still in the courtyard. He had not climbed back into it yet, and of all things, he was standing there, having a conversation with Mrs. Hawthorne. Neither of them looked particularly annoyed at it either. No, not even Mrs. Hawthorne.

I might have taken more time to observe and ponder over the remarkable sight in other circumstances. But as things were, I only had a mind to ask him if he would put in to dispatch a stagecoach to retrieve me early the next morning. Isolated as Bristlewood Manor was from town, Mr. Havisham was often quite willing to perform light errands for us, so long as we slipped him a few coins, which I did. Mr. Havisham tipped his hat to me and said it would be done, and I thanked him profusely.

Mrs. Hawthorne stared at me with curiosity but didn't say anything. I felt no need to explain myself to her just then.

I returned to the house, and I am unabashed to admit that I was thereupon reduced to bitter tears. Unlike Halifax, I had been fortunate in that I was relatively unacquainted with death at that point in my life, and the prospect of losing my mother forever was grueling. As much as I hated the thought of leaving Halifax to make a temporary trip back home, I was desperate for one more opportunity to speak with her and hold her before she died.

And anyway, I knew that Halifax, of all people in the world, would understand that.

Sitting back down in the drawing room, I let myself cry alone. Halifax was not there, as I've said, and that was actually preferable, as it allowed me to cope with the shock of the news myself before sharing it with him. Once I had composed myself somewhat, I went upstairs with heavy limbs and a runny nose to ask him for a leave of absence, expecting it to be no issue whatsoever, which was why I had already ordered the stagecoach.

"Mr. Fairfield?" I called out in the corridor of his apartment. That was the appellation by which I still called him whenever we were outside of his bedroom, as we sought to maintain some sense of public-facing propriety.

There was no answer from anywhere on the second floor. I checked both the bedroom and the room with the mirror, but he was not there. So, I knocked on the door of his study, presuming he must be inside it.

"Mr. Fairfield?" I repeated.

Again, there was no response. Neither did I hear the sounds of movement within.

"Halifax? Are you all right?"

Growing suddenly, and perhaps unnecessarily, concerned that something horrible had happened to him, I put my hand on the knob and threw open the door. This room was still off-limits to me then, but I figured he would forgive my trespassing under the circumstances.

But he was not in there either.

I was, of course, relieved to find that he had not collapsed unconscious on the floor, but unless he had slipped out to relieve himself, I didn't know where he could have gone.

I stepped into the study, irresistibly intrigued by this forbidden chamber, even despite the horrible news I had just received. After all, while I respected his need for solitude, I didn't like being excluded from certain areas of his home, especially when I'd already probed every part of his body. What more could he have to hide from me that I hadn't already come to intimately know anyway?

And so, I entered.

The room, like the rest of the second floor, was sparsely furnished, and he had apparently not been too uptight about dusting. There was only an old sofa placed along the near wall and a wooden desk and chair installed under the window, which had had the curtains drawn over it, darkening the space. A book sat atop the desk, and I wondered if Halifax had been further practicing his reading while he was alone. That would have been quite charming, but why the secrecy then?

Curious to see what the book was, I approached the desk. It was old, thick, and bound in black leather, and it wasn't one I recognized. I picked it up, feeling its hefty weight in my hands, and then peeled back the cover and the flyleaf.

I nearly shrieked at what I read on the title page.

*Grimoire of the Dead.*

I prayed that this was merely one of those horror novels with a misleading and terrifying name. But as I thumbed through its pages, I beheld, to my titanic dread and dismay, that it was exactly what it appeared to be. Each chapter was a thorough instruction on how to perform all manner of ghastly magical rites, of which, I believed, no upstanding person should have partaken. Even a passing, academic interest in that kind of subject matter seemed, to me, reprehensible.

A chill passed through my body. What on earth could Halifax be doing with a book like this? With the large library in the drawing room downstairs, there was no shortage of honorable reading options. Why was *this* the one he chose to peruse in his alone time?

It was then that I noticed the improvised bookmark inserted about two-thirds of the way through the text's pages. With shaking fingers, I flipped to the flagged spot.

This time, I did gasp aloud upon reading the chapter's title: "The Reanimation of the Dead."

"What the devil are you doing?"

I hadn't heard Halifax's approach, and when he spoke in that angry voice, it made me jump and cry out. He stood there in the open doorway, his blue eyes glaring and furious, his jaw coiled tight.

"I was looking for you," I said in a frail, trembling voice, hoping my alibi would appease him. I let the book close, but I held onto it. "I need to request a leave of absence from you. I received a letter from my father today. It seems my mother has fallen ill, and they require me at home. It does not look good. My father expects that she may die within a week's time."

"I'm sorry to hear that," replied Halifax, although his tone belied the reality that he didn't feel any sympathy for me right then. Not when he had caught me red-handed like this. "But that is no excuse for entering a room I have expressly forbidden you to enter."

Remembering the tome in my hands and my visceral aversion to it, I held it up to him. "Is this why you forbade me to come in here? To keep me from finding this awful thing?"

"It is none of your concern," he returned firmly and flatly.

"How do you figure?" I spat back. Now, I felt myself becoming enraged as well, both at his apparent lack of compassion for me and at his study of this book. "Is it not my right to know if my employer and the master of the house in which I reside is practicing sorcery?"

"I am not practicing sorcery," he asserted, walking toward me and snatching the book from my hands. He pointed at the door. "Now, get out of here at once."

"I will not," I proclaimed, settling my feet in that spot and staring back at him defiantly. "Not until you tell me what you have been doing up here with a book like that."

"It is none of your concern," he repeated, his inflection dangerously calm. "Get out of here at once, lest I shall have to throw you out myself.

"Come on, Halifax," I pleaded. "Considering everything that has happened between us, I deserve to know why you have that horrible thing."

"It is none of your concern!" he snapped before taking in a deep, stuttering inhale to regain himself.

"The practice of witchcraft is the concern of any decent, God-fearing person," I said with conviction.

But Halifax laughed acerbically at me. "Oh, honestly, Edwin!" he cried. "Do you seriously mean to suggest that you, of all people, are a decent, God-fearing person? You, who shoves your prick into another man's asshole every chance you get? You, who spends like a geyser and moans like a cheap whore? Decent and God-fearing, my foot!"

The cruel calculation behind that attack made me positively livid. "How dare you mock me!" I barked, shaking with wrath of my own. "After holding me and helping me through my terrors, you now condescend to ridicule me? You are a spineless coward, Mr. Fairfield! How dare you!"

He was perfectly unaffected by my words. "And how dare you enter this room with the full knowledge that you were never to set foot inside?" he riposted. "Did my care and concern for you not earn me the right to a bit of privacy? Or are you now the master of the house?"

I pretended as if I hadn't heard him. And anyway, I almost didn't hear him, because new, harrowing ideas had entered my mind.

"Your mother's grave," I wheezed faintly. "Did you rob your mother's grave? Did you hire me to teach you to read so you could go through that text and revive your mother's corpse?"

I didn't necessarily believe what I was saying, but I couldn't avoid entertaining the suspicion.

His eyes flashed white hot at the allegation. "You are a delusional lunatic!" he roared violently. "My mother's grave is untouched, and you know it. I refuse to stand here and allow a hysterical man like you to hurl the most outrageous accusations at me in my own house!"

"I take that to mean you have granted my leave of absence from your service, Mr. Fairfield?" I asked sardonically.

"Indeed, I have," he sneered. "And do not concern yourself with arranging a return trip, Mr. Hayward. Your employment at Bristlewood Manor is at an end."

Hot tears sprung into my eyes at that last bit, but I didn't argue with him or beg for his mercy. My honor wouldn't let me, nor would my reason or my sense of morality. I had not, in all honesty, expected this arrangement to last forever, and given this fresh intelligence about Halifax's character, there was no conceivable way that I could continue with him. If he hadn't dismissed me, I would have quit myself.

So, with one last, blurry look at him, I stormed out of the room and out of his life, suddenly regretting that I had ever known him.

# CHAPTER TWENTY-THREE

All the guilt and shame I should have experienced throughout the past two weeks collapsed upon me with devastating force the moment I entered my third-floor bedroom. With indescribable horror, I clearly saw how far I had strayed from that narrow way "which findeth life," and I feared my feet may never make their way back to it again.

I fell to my knees just as I had a fortnight before, and, with my fingers interlocked and tightly clamped, I begged God for his bountiful forgiveness. I vowed that I would never again commit the sins I had so flagrantly perpetrated during the last two weeks if he would only pardon me.

Never mind the fact I had made that promise before and, having utterly failed in keeping it, had ended up in this situation once again.

"Lord Jesus Christ, son of God, have mercy on me, a sinner," I wailed at the top of my lungs, not caring who overheard me. "Lord Jesus Christ, son of God, have mercy on me, a sinner. Lord Jesus Christ, son of God, have mercy on me, a sinner. Lord Jesus Christ, son of God, have mercy on me, a sinner. Lord Jesus Christ, son of God, have mercy on me, a sinner. Lord Jesus Christ, son of God, have mercy on me, a sinner."

"Sinnersinnersinnersinner!"

Ah, finally. Mr. William had returned once more, his accusations louder and stronger than ever.

And more deserved, too.

"Leave me alone!" I cried.

"Sinnersinnersinnersinner!"

I screamed out for deliverance, but there was none to be had, neither from God nor from Halifax. I had been abandoned to the consequences of my iniquity. This was the natural fate of a degenerate man like me. And I was degenerate in the truest sense of the word, for I had not simply made a mistake once and learned from it. I did not do as the Lord Jesus commanded the woman caught in adultery to do when he said to "go, and sin no more." No. On the contrary, I had habitually committed the same disgraceful sin over and over again, without remorse, without regret, without shame, and without repentance. Like the people of Israel and Judah, I'd had several chances to turn back, several chances to change my ways, several chances to submit to the Lord in contrition; but I had persisted in my waywardness. I had become a wanton offender, and as a result, I had no doubt cast myself beyond the reach of grace and redemption.

You may argue that no one is too far gone, that there is no sinner who cannot yet become a saint. But I say to you that if that were the case, there would be no such thing as hell. My body may have still been breathing, but my soul may as well have already been thrown into the lake of fire.

There was nothing to be done.

And so, I got up and lay down on the bed, deciding to relax into the reckoning. I was reaping what I had sowed. There could be no escaping it, so why even try?

"Sinnersinnersinnersinner!" said Mr. William.

"Sinnersinnersinnersinner!" I replied.

If he was surprised by my change in tone, he did not show it, for he simply responded in kind. In fact, we maintained an almost pleasant back-and-forth conversation like that until, rather than a nuisance, the voice of Mr. William became something like a dear friend to me, the kind that keeps you grounded. I was a sinner, after all, and a particularly infamous one at that, so we had a great deal about which we could agree.

It didn't cross my mind to consider how very much like a madman that behavior made me seem. And perhaps that, in and of itself, was the exemplary trait of the genuine madman.

I quit my blubbering, and eventually, an irenic numbness came over me. There was something almost freeing in the acceptance of what I was. But dear reader, do not suspect that, in that dispassionate acceptance, I had found a license to continue in sin. In believing I was destined for and deserving of eternal conscious torment, I couldn't simply allow myself to flagrantly mock the laws of God while I still had the time to do so. My punishment, I intended, would not dally until after my death, but it would instead commence right then with the rest of my life spent in self-abnegation. With my mother's death imminent, I would become a dutiful son to my family, a respectable member of the community, and a bleeding heart for the poor and needy.

And when I breathed my last, I would, with poise, welcome the flames.

I calmly packed up my belongings save for a nightshirt to sleep in and a set of clothes for the morning. Mr. Havisham was kind enough to send a messenger to the house, who confirmed that a stagecoach would pick me up first thing on the morrow. That was good. I wanted to be away from Bristlewood Manor as soon as possible, before I had to see Halifax again. I would not seek a rapprochement with him, seeing no possible benefit in that. I simply needed to put this place behind me right away, to put Halifax behind me right away.

I now knew him for what he truly was: a demonic tempter with lurid interests and desires. His words and his presence had seemed so sweet and comforting to me, but that was as it always was with enchanters like him. The serpent in the garden, though still a serpent, had conducted himself in a duplicitously sensible and benevolent manner; otherwise, his blandishments would have borne no fruit. So it was with Halifax. He had tickled my ear (and other parts of my body) with his forked tongue, and he had led me into a life of decadence and abasement. I didn't blame him for my crimes, though; "the devil made me do it" is a defense that never holds up in the courts of man or heaven. I simply recognized that anything like love I had felt for him had only been based on a damnable lie.

Did I honestly believe that then? I don't know and can't say. But it's what I told myself if for no other reason than to make our leave-taking less hellish on me. It's so much easier to leave someone if you can convince yourself that they are a villain, and that is what I endeavored to do.

However, it pained me to think of Halifax in that manner. Whatever my feelings about him now were, there was still a softness for him in my heart. I interpreted that as pity rather than love; after all, the satan had taken advantage of Halifax's tragic circumstances and hoodwinked him into all sorts of heterodox beliefs about God and human sexuality. Halifax, I knew, wasn't a scoundrel at heart, but the devil had taken hold of him and made him into an agent of hell, defiling not just himself, but others as well. Namely, me.

I passed the remainder of that evening taking a final stroll through Bristlewood Manor and the grounds surrounding it. Mr. William did not allow me the freedom of mind to contemplate whether or not I would miss the mansion, and maybe that was for the best. Coming here in the first place had been a horrendous mistake, I now knew. My parents had tried to warn me, and the strangeness of the letter that had called me thence should have alerted me to it long before that final night.

Oh, well. Fortunately, I had only sunk a few weeks in that place. I still had plenty of life ahead of me, and I would spend the entirety of it atoning for my brief time at Bristlewood Manor.

It was such a tremendous shame that I had spent the last weeks of my mother's life in such evil. It was hard to evade the thought that somehow my crimes had caused her illness. If anything, it should've been my health that failed.

With an early start planned for the morrow, I retired to my bed just after night had fallen, the smell of incoming rain carried on the breeze. Mr. William sang me to sleep, and it was a bizarre, if effective, lullaby.

"Sinnersinnersinnersinner!"

# CHAPTER TWENTY-FOUR

I awoke to the same old screaming, although it was the first time I'd heard it in two weeks. However, there was neither frantic gasping for breath nor a furiously racing heart. There was only the feeling of fatalistic inevitability. Why should my last night at Bristlewood Manor feature anything other than an encore of its most beloved ballads?

"Ahh– ahh – ahh – ahh – ahh – ahh – ahh – ahh – ahh – ahh–."

"Sinnersinnersinnersinner!"

What an incredible harmony those two cries made, representing, as they did, the two belligerents at war within me! Indeed, it did strike me as almost beautiful in some way, although it deterred me from returning to sleep, particularly when rendered in combination with the thunderstorm rolling in outside.

I needed my rest, what with the early start and the dire situation to which I would soon return home. However, all that racket would make sleep impossible.

Well, the screaming had been quieter when I had gone down to the drawing room before, even if it had all been in my head. Therefore, I suspected I might be able to regain my slumber if I reposed on the sofa one last time. Just as long as Halifax didn't burst in the door from digging up another grave, or whatever it was he had been doing that night.

Getting up from bed, I lit a candle and creeped out of my bedroom in my nightclothes. An almost pleasant sense of deja vu came over me.

As I passed through the second floor, I wondered if the howling was another hallucination or if Halifax was masturbating in front of his mirror again now that we had separated. I didn't care enough to investigate. I didn't want to see him at all, and I especially didn't want to see him like that.

But, of course, at the same time, that was all I wanted right then. I wanted to see him, to hold him, to kiss him, to strip him naked, to suck his cock, to lick his asshole, and so many other things.

However, I grappled with the temptation, and this time, I conquered it. I could even consider him with patronizing sympathy. That poor soul. He was so unaware of how he was condemning and demeaning himself with each stroke of his luscious prick.

When I came to the bottom of the stairs, I found that Mrs. Hawthorne was in the drawing room, still dressed from the day and engaged in some needlework by the light of an oil lamp.

"Oh, I'm so sorry, Mrs. Hawthorne," I said, stepping back in surprise at her unexpected presence there. "I didn't realize you were still up."

She promptly set aside her needlework and looked me over in my nightclothes. "Come on in, Mr. Hayward," she said, apparently neither startled nor bothered by my sudden appearance. She didn't even seem generally irritated. "And please, do sit down. I would like to speak with you for a moment."

That was odd; Mrs. Hawthorne had never wanted to speak to me before. But I did as I was told, sitting across from her on the sofa I'd been on when I first saw Halifax, when I was first struck by his winsome good looks.

The wailing – as well as Mr. William's constant allegations – had stopped.

I almost missed them.

"I understand you are leaving this morning," said Mrs. Hawthorne as thunder rumbled, lightning flashed, and rain pattered on the windowpane.

"That's correct," I replied stiffly. "My mother is ill, and I desire to spend her final days with her."

She stared at me perceptively, as if she could read my mind. "And you plan to not return to Bristlewood Manor." It was not a question. She already knew.

"No, I do not plan to return," I confirmed.

With a cryptic sigh, Mrs. Hawthorne picked up her needlework again and continued where she'd left off. "Did you know that I was there when Mr. Fairfield was born? Mr. Halifax Fairfield, that is."

I shook my head at her, although it was no great challenge to imagine it considering her age and her long employment at Bristlewood Manor. But I wondered what had driven her to bring up this subject unprompted now, especially in the context of her prior circumvention of my questions. It seemed like she would've just been glad to hear I was leaving and kept to herself until I was finally gone.

But as it turned out, she had a story to tell.

"I never had any children of my own, but he was as close to being my own as any child could have been," she went on, her hands slowing as she fell into a flight of nostalgia. "I fell in love with him the moment I first saw him. He was such a lovely, happy child. Even as an infant, he rarely cried. Not unless he needed something specific, and I was always quick to provide it to him. I wasn't the housekeeper then. I was his nurse, and there was no greater satisfaction in my life than that occupation. His radiant blue eyes captivated everyone who met him, and it was impossible for anyone not to love him. He was a bright, well-behaved, and polite boy, well on his way to becoming a fitting future master of Bristlewood Manor.

"I know he told you about why his father sent him away. That, I must own, is the single greatest regret of my life. You see, it was me who found those horrible drawings in his bedroom. Perhaps I shouldn't call them horrible, but you will understand my meaning, I imagine. At the time, they seemed so horrible to me, even if I've grown in my understanding since then. Well, anyway, I was so offended by them that I went right to his father to show them to him. I never meant for Mr. Halifax to be brutalized as a result. But Mr. William was so livid. I was there to witness it myself. I saw how Mr. William beat him so severely. Mr. William almost looked like a demon as he flogged his own son far beyond what I felt even a hardened, incorrigible criminal deserved. I couldn't contain my tears at that moment, and Mr. William ordered me out of the room forthwith.

"When it was finally over, and when Mr. Halifax had been confined to his room, I flew up to him to beg for his forgiveness. He offered it freely, but I don't think he really knew the gravity of what I'd done. He was just a child. I will never forget how those big tears fell from his beautiful blue eyes as he wept in physical and emotional pain. He didn't understand the whole situation, but he did understand that his father believed something very vile about him. And, at that age, you know, if his father believed it, then, to him, it must have been true.

"That experience transformed me, Mr. Hayward, just as it transformed Mr. Halifax, although in very different ways, I suppose. Mr. William's bloodthirsty anger was based in the dictates of scripture, he claimed, and was, therefore, justified. I was scandalized by that, much more so than I had been by Mr. Halifax's drawings. And over time, I realized that if holy writ could ordain such terrible violence, then I could not accept it as inerrant truth. That belief only became more ingrained in me when Mr. William shipped Mr. Halifax off to Antigua with his uncle, and when he repeatedly refused to let him return, even against Mrs. Amelia's imploring. I felt as if the entire ordeal had been my fault; if I had just ignored the child's drawings, if I had just dismissed them as the doodles of a little boy, none of this would have happened.

"And so, I determined that I would do whatever I had to do in order to earn Mr. Halifax's forgiveness in adulthood, when he had a greater comprehension of the situation. I should point out that he readily forgave me when he came home upon inheriting Bristlewood Manor. So deep was his forgiveness, in fact, that I was the only one to maintain employment here upon his return, though that is not to say that the other servants had been dismissed out of any animosity. But anyway, my object then changed from doing whatever I could to earn his forgiveness to doing whatever I could to ensure his happiness, for his life to that point had been so bereft of any of that.

"Now, I may be just an old lady, but I am not incapable of accepting new and even shocking ideas. I made certain that Mr. Halifax knew I loved him no matter what, and that I affirmed his love for others in whatever form it took. That is a blasphemous and sacrilegious thing for me to do, perhaps, but compared to the vicious abuse of Mr. William, no form of genuine love could strike me as anything approaching wickedness.

"And then, you showed up here. I didn't take to you myself, but, for whatever reason, Mr. Halifax did. And powerfully, too. But I knew he loved you before he even knew it himself. I saw it in the way his eyes lit up whenever he beheld you, in the way he sat so close to you during your lessons, in the way he strived so arduously to please you with his learning. I knew it all. You may have thought I didn't notice that you two have been sleeping in the same room, but I did. I'm not quite as senile as I might seem. And I know this in my very soul: you have brought him more happiness in your short time here than he's ever had in his life, and that has pleased me very much.

"But now, Mr. Hayward, you are planning to leave Bristlewood Manor. Mr. Halifax did not explain to me what his quarrel was with you, and I don't need to know. It is none of my concern. But as he told me about your impending removal, what was evident to me was his piercing regret and his immense heartbreak. And that broke my heart as well, as much of a nuisance as I find you to be. I urged him to reconcile with you, but he said that he didn't think you would ever forgive him. It seems his father's behavior toward him has led him to believe he's unforgivable.

"I don't know myself the kind of man you are at heart, Mr. Hayward, but I'm assured that if Mr. Halifax loves you, then you must be very, very good indeed. I only pray that you will pardon his error, whatever it was, and go to him straight away. I have seen in you a love that is not based on fortunes or social standing or familial pressure, but on honest, genuine affection and care. I'm not an expert on these things, but to me, that is a truer love than most any you will find these days. Don't waste it. Go to him. You deserve one another."

Her story had brought me to weeping. Mrs. Hawthorne had so deeply moved me that I felt I could forgive any wrongdoing on Halifax's part. I wouldn't – I couldn't – be the kind of brute Mr. William had been. Halifax deserved to know he could be forgiven and loved.

To hear that I had been the source of the greatest joy in his life was humbling, and it brought me to the realization that he had been the source of mine. Perhaps he had been a Delilah, seducing me in order to bring about my ruin. Perhaps my loving him was the lowest of sins and would lead to hideous punishments in the hereafter. Suddenly, none of that seemed to matter very much to me. All my life, my worst fear had been a future hell; however, now, my worst fear was a present hell. And an existence without love, an existence without Halifax, would have certainly been a present hell. I couldn't understand how I'd so willingly consigned myself to such a life before.

"I will go to him," I said through my sobs, unashamed to let her see me like that. Shame was such a wasted energy. "I will go to him right now. Is he in bed?"

"No," she replied, shaking her head. "He is out. I believe he is in the old privy behind the mansion."

I'd seen the old privy during my walks out on the grounds, but it had been so squalid and tightly locked up that I had assumed no one had been inside of it in decades. What on earth would Halifax be doing in there?

But I didn't care what he was doing. I had to see him immediately. I had to tell him how I felt and apologize for hurting him and forgive him for any of his misdeeds.

"Thank you, Mrs. Hawthorne," I cried, standing up and going over to kiss her cheek. "Thank you so much."

She only responded with a smile. I'd never seen that from her before, at least not for anyone besides Halifax. It suited her quite nicely.

# CHAPTER TWENTY-FIVE

It may've been wise to have gotten dressed or at least put on shoes before rushing off in search of Halifax, but my haste wouldn't allow it. The rain had made the ground outside muddy and wet, and the grime caked my bare feet and the hem of my nightclothes. I paid it no mind whatsoever, and I sprinted as fast as I could through the raging storm toward the old privy where I would find the man I loved. The wind moaned and pushed back on me, but I proved stronger in my tenacity. Nothing was going to stop me from getting to him.

As I approached the dilapidated shack, I tried to craft what my speech to Halifax ought to be. I had to be persuasive and concise, as I may not have much time to speak before he cast me out from his presence. However, I could not think of actual words to form my argument. I could only think of my love for him and of my willingness to throw myself at his feet to beg for his clemency.

Hopefully, that would be enough to convince him to take me back in his arms again.

"Sinnersinnersinnersinner!" seethed Mr. William as I ran. He was furious at this turn of events and particularly chafed by my intention to express and ask for forgiveness.

"Go rot in hell, you miserable old bastard!" I replied.

And it seemed as if he did.

I didn't pause to knock upon reaching the privy. Seeing the key in the latch was turned to its unlocked position, I immediately burst through the rickety door. It swung wide open and slammed into the interior side of the front wall with a loud *bang*.

Inside, I found Halifax, still fully dressed in the clothes he had been wearing the last time I saw him. He was bent over a table, studying something intently.

But he spun around when I entered, his eyes wide with shock and alarm.

"What the devil is this?" he exclaimed, frantically spreading out his arms to disguise whatever was happening on the table behind him.

"Halifax!" I cried. "I must speak with you. I —"

However, my voice trailed off when my attention was tersely ripped away from him and cast upon what he'd failed to hide. On that table, I beheld the most grotesque, sickening monstrosity I could have ever imagined.

It was a fetid, decaying corpse, complete with a burial gown and a decomposing head of wispy, rust-colored locks. The neck was slightly and pervertedly cocked to the right. Leaned against the body was *Grimoire of the Dead*, open to that horrid chapter where the bookmark had been earlier in the day.

Then I noticed the mephitic stench that infested the shack, assaulting my nostrils, poisoning my lungs, and twisting my stomach. Between the sight and the smell, I doubled over in staggering disgust and began to retch before I could say anything more.

Upon seeing me otherwise incapacitated, Halifax launched straight into action, not waiting around to hear what I had to say whenever I regathered myself. He twisted back to the table and hoisted the body over his shoulder, gripping it there with one hand. Then, he grabbed a lit lantern and moved toward the door, abandoning *Grimoire of the Dead* on the table.

Swallowing my queasiness, I tried to follow him, but with the fist holding the lantern, he shoved my flailing body onto the dusty wood floor.

I sat up just in time to see him pull open the door and turn back to me with a despondent look in those blue eyes. "I'm sorry," he breathed.

And then he went out into the tempest, shutting the door behind him and locking me inside the privy. He'd previously spoken of a desire to free me from my spiritual prison, but now, he'd trapped me in a physical one.

"No!" I shrieked, jumping to my feet and smashing my body into the door, which did not budge against my weight. "Halifax! Come back! Come back!"

But he didn't come back, no matter how much I screamed and cried. I vomited on the floor, the putrid redolence of death still squelching the air.

After dispatching the entirety of my last meal, I pressed my face into the door, overcome by horror, nausea, and dejection. The scene hadn't lasted more than fifteen seconds, but I relived it over and over in my mind, particularly the way Halifax had so insouciantly touched that carcass with his bare hands and threw me on the ground like a rag doll.

Collapsing to my ass on the floor with my back flattened against the door, I fully grasped the situation at hand. I had taken Halifax at his word when he'd explained the grime all over him that night he came in the back door. He'd said it had been the result of an accidental fall. That had been the evening before Mrs. Hawthorne found Mrs. Amelia's grave had been robbed. And while I had briefly suspected something unseemly then, I couldn't honestly believe that someone so generous and attentive could have effectuated something so nefarious. Even when I found *Grimoire of the Dead* in his private study, I hadn't truly thought he would actually attempt to revive his mother's carcass.

Apparently, though, that was exactly what he'd been trying to do, and I was a captive in this outhouse, unable to stop him, unable to do anything but sob.

But at my core, I understood his motivation for doing it. Grief can compel people to make all sorts of confounding decisions, and digging up his mother's dead body and attempting to reanimate it was certainly confounding. However, it was also utterly abominable, and it could only end in emotional devastation at best and some unspeakable atrocity at worst.

I had to appraise, just then, whether I still loved Halifax, whether I could disregard this outrageous scandal, or whether I could at least continue to love him in spite of it.

It may strike you as hopelessly naive and cretinous that the answer I settled on was yes. Halifax had been so solicitous of me in my time of distress, and this, as uncivilized as he was behaving, was indubitably his time of distress. His father hadn't forgiven him, but I would. I had to be there for him, come what may. And I fully expected something horrible to come.

That meant I couldn't stay in the privy. Thankfully, it was such an ancient, ramshackle building that I was sure it could not contain me for long.

With a mix of desperation, love, and terror, I clambered up to my feet and propelled myself at the door, crushing my shoulder into it. It didn't open, and it left my shoulder throbbing, but I heard the cracking of wood and felt it give a little. So I repeated the action. This time, the door sprung open with a loud, splintering snap, and I went careening out of the shack, landing on my face in a puddle of mud.

# CHAPTER TWENTY-SIX

Pain registered somewhere in my consciousness, but it wasn't enough to keep me from scrambling up to my feet right away. I was soiled all over with filth now, and I had to wipe off my face before I could open my eyes. Even when I did, the night was so dark that the only illumination came from the oil lamp guttering in the privy, the few lights still lit in the house, and the occasional bursts of lightning.

I couldn't see Halifax anywhere, and I had no idea where he would have gone with a corpse heaved over his shoulder.

But I stomped through the mud in search of him regardless. The rain soaked me to the bone, clearing off some of the mud from my face, but otherwise, I hardly noticed it.

"Halifax!" I cried, even though I highly doubted he would answer me. Not when I recalled the determination with which he had picked up that body, pushed me down, and fled from the outhouse. "Halifax! Where are you? Halifax!"

He could have gone anywhere on the expansive grounds of Bristlewood Manor. Without a light and unable to use the lamp in the outhouse because of the rain, I raced around to the front of the outhouse. There were gaslights there, so I could rule that out easily enough before having to search in the dark.

As I ran, I begged for aid from whatever deities might have approved of my love for Halifax. I didn't know if any such entities existed, but it wouldn't hurt to try. The Christian God probably wouldn't have granted me anything, but at that moment, I was willing to accept help from the God of any religion.

Someone must have been listening to my pleas, for I realized my prayers had been answered when I reached the front of the house.

There, in the courtyard of Bristlewood Manor, I found Halifax, lit up by his lantern and a row of gas lamps.

As I came closer, bellowing his name at the top of my lungs, the scene came into clearer view. He had set the corpse on its feet and tied it around the middle to one of the lampposts with his shirt. Meanwhile, fluttering in the air above that lamppost and anchored to it was a kite, which was buffeted on all sides yet kept afloat by the turbulent gales of the storm. Bare-chested and turned away from me, Halifax stood a good ten feet in front of the body, facing it with his arms reached toward the heavens. The muscles in his back shimmered in the rain and the gaslight, and his bony fingers formed into claws. He was yelling something I couldn't make out, but it sounded crazed and desperate.

"Halifax!" I shrieked.

Either he did not hear me or he ignored me, so I quit vociferating and focused on just getting to him.

When I had come within twenty feet of him, I was stopped dead in my tracks by the vision of something that could have only been the gimmick of gothic horror fiction, something that has occasionally haunted my dreams since then. I will understand if you do not believe what I'm about to describe. If I hadn't seen it with my own eyes, I would have never believed it either.

A blinding bolt of lightning lashed down from the sky and crashed into the kite with a loud snap. It sent a sizzling beam of electricity down through the kite's wire, down through the gaslight pole, and into the corpse. But rather than bursting into flames, which I would have expected, the body convulsed for a few chilling moments.

Then it broke loose from its binding and somehow took flight, hovering surreally in the air a few feet above the ground.

It made a direct course for Halifax, coming to a stop a mere three feet in front of him. He didn't run away or even seem shocked by what he saw.

This was what he'd wanted. He'd done it. In some way, by some awful witchcraft, he'd revived his mother's carcass. However, the body was stiff, putrescent, and still quite dead as it floated in front of Halifax.

Was this what he'd expected? Or had he anticipated her to return just as she had been in life?

I didn't have time to ponder those questions further, for in a turn of events more execrable than any of the preceding horrors, Mrs. Amelia's lower jaw opened.

"Oh, my son," said the carcass in a demented and grating, yet vaguely feminine, voice. "My dear, sweet son."

"Mamma!" cried Halifax, reaching out for the body but unable to touch it, as if his feet had been cemented to the ground.

"Your love for me is powerful, my son," the corpse went on in that abominable accent, despite the sweetness of its words, "and my love for you is eternal. But it cannot be resurrected from the grave. The past is the past. Seek love now, my dear son, where it may still be found."

And then, before Halifax could respond, the deceased body of Mrs. Amelia Fairfield shot up into the sky, angling behind me toward Bristlewood Manor.

I spun around and saw it had halted in front of a second-story window, the one in Halifax's study The corpse stared at the panes as if lost in a reverie, almost like it was remembering its final moments of true life.

I could almost imagine the scene that had transpired there three and a half years ago: Mrs. Amelia, so overcome with the grief of her estranged son and the cruelty of her husband, looking out from that window with a rope around her neck, preparing to jump because she had no other option. Did she know that, at the desk beneath that window, her son would one day learn the black art of bringing her back from the dead? Did she know how much he loved her? Did she know the deranged lengths to which he would go to get her back again?

In some part of my heart, I hoped she did. Perhaps her soul – wherever it was, whether encased in that body or up in heaven – was watching right then, acknowledging the noble intentions of her son, if not approving of his actions. I could never denigrate her decision to end her life, but I longed for her to be aware that Halifax loved her so very deeply.

And that I loved him too.

Suddenly, the carcass continued its flight again, rocketing straight up into the air. When it reached an altitude of one hundred feet or so, it exploded into a million tiny pieces that never seemed to settle, vanishing as if it had never been there in the first place.

If I had not already thrown up a few minutes earlier, I very well would have done so again. None of my unhinged delusions had been anywhere near the repulsiveness of that grisly sight.

"No!" screeched Halifax from behind me, the grief making his vocalization crack like an adolescent.

I turned back to him. Freed from his unseen shackles, he kicked his lantern, shattering it and sending it flying fifteen feet away.

"No!" he repeated. "Mamma! Mamma! I need you! Mamma! Come back! Mamma!"

Frozen where I stood, I could hardly process what I had just witnessed. But nonetheless, I began to weep as I listened to this lost boy mourn the loss of his mother afresh. Horribly misguided as he had been, his experiment had been an earnest endeavor to reanimate the love that had been ripped away from him at too young of an age.

And it had utterly failed.

Like the small boy he'd been the last time he'd seen his mother alive, Halifax pounded his feet in fury and appeared as if he were looking for something else to kick or throw or otherwise destroy. Finding nothing, he ripped off his shoes and socks and chucked them as far as he could. Then, incredibly, he rent his pants right off his legs, the fabric ripping like paper. He tore the trousers into several pieces, flung the destroyed article to the ground, and trampled it into the mud beneath his bare feet, the only pathetic, puerile way for him to express his acute anguish.

Finally, he collapsed onto his knees with his back to me, completely naked and sobbing like a baby who simply needed his mother's embrace for comfort.

But it would not come, and it never would again. It was gone forever. Even the profane hope of bringing her back from the dead had deserted him.

And then, I remembered my own mother, whose death appeared imminent, and my heart swelled with immense sorrow.

That broke me out of my trance. I ran up to him, slipping a bit in the mud as I did, and grabbed him in my arms, falling to my knees beside him. However, aside from jolting slightly with the impact of our bodies, he seemed not even to recognize my presence.

"Halifax!" I yelled at him, hugging his slippery, dripping body close to me. "Halifax, it's me! It's Edwin! I'm here, Halifax! Talk to me! Please, Halifax!"

But he just continued to stare straight ahead, his eyes dead and vacuous like he'd seen a ghost. Or like he'd become one himself, leaving his body lifeless and void.

"Halifax, please!" I groaned into his ear as I forcefully shook him and kissed his cheeks. "Please, answer me! I need you!"

Though he still breathed and I could feel his heartbeat under my hands, there was practically no other sign of life to be found in him. It was like his spirit had gone away forever, like his soul had escaped from this world to be with his beloved mother, wherever she was now.

But I wouldn't let him go. I couldn't. Not after everything Mrs. Hawthorne had said. Not after everything I had just seen. Not with all the love I had for him, which filled me so totally that I thought I, too, might spontaneously combust.

Rattling and yelling at him had not worked, though. I needed to undertake an alternative tactic. But what could I do?

The only possibility that entered my brain was truly ludicrous, and I had no substantive suspicion it would even be effective. But love for his mother had led Halifax to do something absurd and, ultimately, ineffective, and in the same way would I let my love for him drive me.

Consequences be damned straight to hell with Mr. William.

Releasing him, I got to my feet and traipsed out so I was directly in front of him at a distance of about ten feet. His eyes didn't betray any indication that they detected me. No matter. I would make him notice me. I had to make him notice me. I had to bring him back to this world, where, as the corpse of his mother had said, love could still be found.

My love.

Grabbing the bottom of my nightshirt, I drew it up over my head, pulled it off, and threw it on the ground between us, leaving me standing completely nude and sopping wet before him. Anyone happening to pass by (unlikely as it was, given the late hour, the storm, and the remoteness of Bristlewould Manor) would have clearly seen me by the gas lamps, and of that shame I was intensely afraid. But compared to my love for Halifax, I may as well have not cared about it at all. I would have paraded myself naked and masturbating in front of the King himself if that would bring back Halifax from this fugue.

I caught a flicker of recognition in his gaze at the sight of me in the buff, but he didn't move or say a word.

So I took it upon myself to speak without any restraint.

"Halifax," I said, nearly shouting to be heard over the rain and the thunder, "I love you. You have redefined everything I thought I knew about myself and the world around me. Before I met you, I only felt immeasurable guilt over who I was and my partiality toward other men. I believed that to act on the latter would have consigned me to an eternity of the worst torment. But you presented to me the inverse of my despair: you revealed to me the beauty of love between two men, and you intoxicated me with it. I used to fear a future of punishment, but now I fear a present without you."

Halifax blinked. His eyes slumped downward to the ground in front of him, and his face twisted in a grimace. Another sign of life, but not enough.

Not yet.

"I love you, Halifax," I went on, grateful for the rain, which disguised my tears, though it could not disguise the emotion in my voice. "I love you more than I ever thought I could love another human being. And now I know that I need you. I'm so sorry for intruding on your private space, and for accusing you of so much wickedness. I failed to see your pain. And I failed to see your need for prodigal love, which is what prompted you to act as you did. I'm so sorry, Halifax. I beg you to forgive me and to allow me to love you until my last breath, for that is what I swear to do, if only you will take me in your arms again. Please, Halifax. Please. I am at your mercy."

He didn't respond to my soliloquy.

At least, not right away.

But after a protracted, painful pause — during which I lost all hope — he suddenly bounded to his feet and closed the space between us with impossible speed. He arrested me in a split second and kissed me so hard it almost hurt.

Almost.

I thrust my lips into his, holding his lovely face between my hands and pressing our naked bodies together. I couldn't have gotten any closer to him without physically becoming a part of his figure. Somehow, I wouldn't have minded that.

He retreated from the kiss after a moment and stared deep into my eyes with his opulent blue irises. The rain continued to pour down on us, but neither of us gave a damn about that.

"I love you, Edwin," he blubbered, pushing my hair out of my face. "My God! I love you so much! But I cannot think of any poetic ways to put it like you did. All I know now is this one thing: I only know that I love you, and I never want to let you go. You are all I have now, and I can't believe I almost let you walk away forever. But I will not let you go again. And I will gladly forgive you if you will forgive me for all this … insanity."

"Of course, I forgive you," I said with a sniveling whimper. I gripped his back so tightly I must have left imprints of my fingers on the skin. "I forgive you as eagerly as I've done anything else in my life. I can't deny that I'm quite … uh, perplexed and disturbed by what I've seen here tonight. But you were there for me in my madness, and I will be here for you in yours."

Halifax let out a laugh and a sob at the same time. "I suppose we're both a little mad, are we not?" he mused.

"If madness is what keeps us together, then I'll gladly be a lunatic," I said, staring into those blue eyes I loved so much.

"I will gladly be a lunatic, too," he repeated with a grin. He fixed me with a clever look. "What do you say we do something a little mad right now?"

I smirked at him diabolically. I understood him implicitly. "Let's see how absolutely mad we can get."

We kissed again with more fanatical zeal than we ever had before. And then, instinctively, we both lay down on the soggy ground beneath the light of the gas lamps.

As usual, our cocks were already hard, and we set right to sucking each other at the same time. After everything we'd been through together, it seemed like there was nothing else we could have done then.

There was something terrifying and electrifying about pleasuring each other right out in the courtyard of Bristlewood Manor, particularly in the midst of a squall. But if someone were to catch us then and we were to be hanged, I would have died a happy madman.

Having Halifax's penis in my mouth was a comfort and a relief as soothing as a soft, warm bed after a strenuous day of work. I had been hours away from leaving him without rectifying our relationship, had so nearly taken a stagecoach away from Bristlewood Manor forever. Ironically, I mused as I slurped him, it was the screaming – whether it had been caused by a ghost or an audible hallucination in my own head – that brought us back together. Had I not been woken up that night, I would have never gone downstairs to speak with Mrs. Hawthorne, and I would have never resolved to seek out Halifax.

What strange twists and turns our lives take! That felt like a particularly apropos observation to make as I sucked his cock in the rain in front of his mansion moments after he'd briefly reanimated his mother's corpse.

After a few minutes of heated mutual fellatio, Halifax got up on his hands and knees, splaying out his ass cheeks to the gaslight and shadows.

I knew what he wanted, and I wanted it too.

Without a word, I moved behind him, brushed the mud out of his crack, and buried my face in his ass, filling his hole with saliva to prepare it for the ineluctable ingress of my throbbing prick. It tasted better than it ever had before somehow, and I couldn't believe I had almost let myself give it up for the rest of my life.

Then, pulling out my head, I loudly smacked his ass with my open hand, adoring the way that cheek vibrated in response.

"That's for being such a naughty boy," I explained, and then I spanked him again.

Halifax crowed at the blow. "I deserved that," he breathed. "But I may need a few more so I can really learn my lesson."

"Oh, I will make sure you know to never try to revive a corpse again," I said, giving him another strike.

It was dark and I didn't have an ideal angle, but I could've sworn I saw a little bit of fluid squirt out of his cock.

After swatting both halves of his rear a few more times, I applied some spit to my tool and stuffed it into him. We both cried out in delight at the act of entry, heedless of the fact that we were outside in full view of the road that passed in front of Bristlewood Manor.

I pounded his ass with a composite of love, lust, and lunacy, and the sound of my crotch slapping against his cheeks echoed happily in the tempestuous night.

Clasping his hair in my fingers, I pulled him up so we were both on our knees, his back pressed to my chest. Then, I dropped my hand down to his wooden phallus and masturbated him as I continued to assail his hole. I caught sight of our thrashing shadows in the glow of the gas lamps, and I reminded myself to suggest to him that we make love in front of his full-length mirror whenever I returned from my trip home. I wanted to see how it looked when I shagged him.

For the first time in any of our sexual soirees to that point – but certainly not for the last – we came at the exact same moment. I spent my seed inside of him, while his semen went flying about the rain-soaked courtyard in huge strands, both of us whooping and hollering.

He swiveled his head around and ensnared me in a corybantic kiss, my cock still in his ass and his still in my hand. A little bit of his come lingered on my fingers.

"My God, how I love you," he moaned into my mouth. "I am mad for you."

"I love you," I returned. "And I am positively mad for you."

A moment later, I pulled out my prick and licked his sperm off my hand. Then we got to our feet, and I struck his ass one more time.

He chuckled.

What a naughty boy he was.

He wrapped his arm around my waist and kissed me. Then we looked back at Bristlewood Manor, still utterly naked and a bit caked in mud.

"I'm so sorry about your mother, Edwin," said Halifax sincerely. "And I'm sorry I had no genuine sympathy for you before. I regret that I let my anger blind me. But you will come back here as soon as you are able, correct?"

"That depends on if I have a job to return to," I said, biting back a smile. "Last I heard, I'd been dismissed from my post as your tutor."

"Of course, you have a job to return to," he told me. "The only thing necessary is for you to accept it."

I turned to him and stared straight into those dazzling eyes. "I happily accept it. As long as I can move out of that tiny bedroom on the third floor and into your bedroom permanently. I sleep so much better when I'm with you."

"I wouldn't have it any other way," he said.

I kissed him, and then we went into Bristlewood Manor — leaving our soiled clothes outside — to wash off the mud from our bodies and get a few hours of sleep before the stagecoach came for me. Thankfully, Mrs. Hawthorne had already gone to bed, although I was certain she would have just been happy that we were back together, no matter what we were or weren't wearing.

I certainly was.

# EPILOGUE

And so, dear reader, I have reached the end of this narrative. My story is, by no means, complete, and perhaps I shall add another volume someday. However, this particular set of salacious and harrowing events worth chronicling for the reading public is now concluded.

But before I lay down my pen for a final time, allow me to leave you with a few brief, closing notes that may be of some interest.

Early the following morning, I departed Bristlewood Manor in a stagecoach bound for home. My mother succumbed to her illness and died two days after my arrival, and I held her hand as she took her final breath. My grief felt illimitable, but I comforted myself with gratitude, thankful that I had the opportunity to spend my mother's last days by her side and to attend her funeral. After all, Halifax never had that chance with Mrs. Amelia.

I didn't speak much to my family about my post at Bristlewood Manor; fortunately for me, the dour mood had dampened any urge for lively, reacquainting conversation. What I did share was brief and simple, mostly related to the work itself. Mrs. Hawthorne proved an entertaining character as well. My tale was obviously bereft of any details regarding my sexual relationship with Halifax, my short descent into madness, or his attempt to reanimate his dead mother. In a private moment, my father asked if I felt it had been a good decision to take up there, and I told him unequivocally that it was. He smiled sadly at me, placed an affectionate hand on my shoulder, and said he was glad to hear it.

Two weeks after my mother had been put in the ground, I returned to my post at Bristlewood Manor with a heavy heart. It was difficult to leave my family, but we all had the responsibility of moving on as best we could. That was what she would have wanted anyway.

Mrs. Hawthorne met me at the door and pressed my hand kindly. Meanwhile, Halifax entwined me in his arms, and we wept together, each mourning our own loss as well as the pain of the other. He was the best commiserator I could have asked for, and while his presence did not heal the hole in my heart, it made the sadness bearable.

When we were all cried out, we were ready for something else. So, we retired to his bedroom – or, I should say, to our bedroom – and stripped off all of our clothes in front of one another. My God, I had missed that naked body of his so much during my absence. Then we kissed, licked, sucked, bit, and rubbed each other all over, reacquainting ourselves with one another using all five of our senses. I even allowed him to infiltrate my ass with his cock (as well as his tongue) for once. Later the same day, I ravished him in front of that full-length mirror, and I came far too soon. It was such a thrill.

Mrs. Hawthorne, though undeniably satisfied that I had reappeared at Bristlewood Manor, didn't necessarily become more pleasant in her interactions with me; however, our banter brought us both such immeasurable diversion that anything else would have been quite disagreeable to each of us.

Halifax quickly became a proficient reader and writer, and I am infinitely indebted to him for editing this text, although there were a few sexual details he demanded I leave out. You can imagine what they were.

About six months after my reinstatement with him, he at last conceded to my constant importunity that he hire more servants to supplement and support Mrs. Hawthorne. He didn't hire a valet, as I gladly added those duties to my charge. Over time, Bristlewood Manor was rehabilitated to its erstwhile splendor, albeit after the fashion of Halifax's and my choosing.

Once we finally got his clothes to a tailor (and he put some more meat on his bones), Halifax became a gentleman of some renown in the area, thrilling new friends with his stories of life in the West Indies and no doubt causing private consternation regarding his mysterious relationship with that Mr. Hayward fellow. I was always with him, after all; some people believed I was simply an overly attentive valet, others presumed I must have been his bastard brother, and, surely, some guessed the true nature of our association.

Of course, there were some young women who were quite smitten by him. How could they not be? He was an incredibly handsome young man with a tremendous fortune and a gargantuan mansion. But, as he had once pointed out to me, "As it turns out, universally acknowledged as that claimed truth may be, not *every* single man in possession of a good fortune is in want of a wife."

He certainly wasn't.

And besides, there was no room in our bed nor our sexual adventures for another person. I was a jealous lover, and so was he.

And now for some of the more brackish details.

With my assistance, Halifax returned his mother's grave to its proper state. We never told Mrs. Hawthorne the truth of the matter, nor did anyone else discover that anything had been amiss. It pained him to know that Mrs. Amelia's coffin was now empty and that it was his own fault. But thankfully, he did not castigate himself for the deed. That isn't to say he excused it either; he fully owned that it was a gruesome bit of misconduct, an errant attempt to dig up (literally) love where it cannot be found. However, he took to heart the words of his revenant mother and resolved to love in the present. I admit I received the majority of that, but it was not just me; Halifax doled out his love to everyone around him, and everyone around him couldn't help but love him back.

Once his mother's grave had been restored, we commissioned and installed three small monuments there to honor Virginia, Sophie, and my own mother, although their bones were buried elsewhere. These were not attempts to return to the past; rather, they were to remind us of what had once been and what had made us who we were, and to cherish what we had now. We visited them often. Sometimes we laughed. Sometimes we cried. But usually, we just held each other while we still could.

Love and loss are inextricable; that is a brutal truth. But for those who have known both, there is an indescribable beauty there too.

You may be curious as to what became of my spiritual life. Well, I began to attend the local church by myself every Sunday. Halifax, who maintained his agnosticism, chose to stay home, and Mrs. Hawthorne, who could not be bothered with being superficially pleasant to so many intolerable people all at once, did so as well. That was fine by me. I still believed in God and I still believed in the Bible, but I no longer ascribed to the conviction that the love between two men was inferior to that which blossomed between a man and a woman. Perhaps we had misinterpreted the text, or perhaps the biblical authors had simply gotten it wrong; regardless, I repudiated the idea that sincere, mutual love could ever be damnable.

I no longer heard screaming at night, unless I was the one mustering it, if you take my meaning. Neither did the voice of Mr. William ever enter my head again. And while Halifax still mourned his mother, it was a grief with which he could live. He burned *Grimoire of the Dead* in the fireplace of our bedroom late one night, thus banishing once and for all the last vestiges of the ghosts of Bristlewood Manor.

Then, right there on the hearth, in front of the blazing flames, I greedily ripped off all his clothes and embedded my cock in his ass. We both screamed in ecstasy, our voices reverberating throughout the room as sweat poured from our bare bodies. The next morning, one of the new servants complained of having been awoken sometime after midnight by the horrid wailing of two ghosts.

# THE END

# About the Author

Percy Popham is the contrived nom de plume for a gay man who wants to write for an audience without his mother finding out about it. He has written many things, most of which are unfinished, and many of which are terrible. When he is not failing at amateur stand-up comedy events or driving around listlessly in tears, he can often be found eulogizing his lost loves to an unwilling listener. He lives, for better or worse, in the United States. His other works are *Providence & Propriety* and *The Officer and the Dandy*. You can find him at @PercyPopham on Twitter and Instagram.

Milton Keynes UK
Ingram Content Group UK Ltd.
UKHW040905100923
428413UK00002B/33